CLUB

ROOM FOUR & ROOM NINE

SIN

MATILDA MARTEL

Cover Design by: Book in it Design, Talina Saine

Edited by Oopsie Daisy Edits

Room Four: Playing with the Big Boys

Club Sin

club
sin

ROOM
FOUR

Playing with the Big Boys.

MATILDA MARTEL

Chapter 1

Jana

Everyone has that one day that changes everything. Some people feel it coming and wake up with black clouds over their heads. They're afraid to get out of bed, fearing doom is around every corner. Others leave the house excited to be alive. Their skin prickles with premonition on the way to work. The universe sends them signs that a life-altering event is just over the horizon, and good or bad, fate will deal her hand.

Today is that day for me.

Unfortunately, I walk into work utterly clueless and head straight into the shitstorm of the century.

Two months in charge, and my board room has turned into chaos. All around me, people ignore my gestures to sit, cast accusations of treachery, and scream profanities at my brothers. It's all well-deserved, but there is a process to these things, and I prefer to maintain order. A few well-intentioned souls make things worse by asking if I'm okay, but my feelings are the least of my worries.

I offer a fake smile and nod. I have nothing more to say. If I speak, I might scream, and if I scream, there's a distinct possibility I will unravel into a hot mess of tears. That is not an option for someone in my position. People depend on me for their jobs. If a member of my staff catches me in a state of despair, they'll panic or do something rash. So, there's no crying in public. The thought alone makes me want to cry, and of course, that only compounds my problem.

While my brothers repeat their apologies and state their case, I gather my portfolio and roll my chair away from the table. There isn't enough air in the room for the three of us, let alone the rest of the board of directors.

"Please, excuse me. I'm leaving for the day." With nothing more on my plate, I rise to my feet and walk to the door, clicking my heels in a perfect storm of anxiety, sadness, and suppressed rage.

As furious as I want to be, I know my brothers did nothing wrong---not technically. The signs were clear, but I stuck my head in the sand like an ostrich, hoping if I didn't address the elephant in the room, it might go away on its own. But it didn't. And I bear responsibility for that.

Once upon a time, Penrose Media ruled the airwaves. We were a powerhouse in print, cable, and digital real estate. But my father's mismanagement, overindulgence, and failure to recognize trends set us behind our competitors. Ever since his death two months ago, we've been treading water upstream and sinking like dead weight.

Jared and Joshua made an executive decision to offer their stock to the highest bidder. I get it. They have to act before word gets out about our financial instability. When that happens, our stock will nosedive into oblivion, and we'll be lucky if we can give it away. Dad left us in a pickle. That's the understatement of the year. If I'm perfectly honest, we're up shit creek without a paddle, and the natives are getting restless.

I can't say that I blame them. If Dad hadn't left me in charge, I might be tempted to do the same thing. But leadership takes guts, and I'm not ready to call it quits.

Charging through the hall like a power walker on speed, I place my hand over my heart and feel it beating like a jackrabbit. When I reach the entrance near my office, I feel dizzy but press on with renewed determination. Behind me, loud thumps distract my pace, and I hear my brother, Jared, call my name. There's no reason to turn because I have nothing to say. I'm too close to the finish line, and I can't waste oxygen giving him a reply.

"I know you hear me, Janie!" Jared's bellow startles me into a sprint, and I slam into my door, fumbling to insert my key like a girl in a slasher film. "Leave me alone, Jared! You no longer have any business here. Leave."

Jared slides behind me, just in time for my confused executive assistant and best friend, Macy, to swing open the door, allowing us to stumble forward together.

"What on God's green earth are you two doing?" I squeeze past her and stagger towards my desk, smoothing out my suit to calm my nerves. "Make him leave, please. I don't want to see him." Jared ignores my pleas and barrels past Macy, who tiptoes past him and tries to make a hasty escape.

I catch her in the act and flash my best pair of puppy dog eyes. "Please, don't go. I need you." I clasp my hands in prayer then point to a chair, begging her not to abandon me too.

"We don't owe him shit, Jana. Dad left this company in shambles and ignored us, especially you, all our lives." He follows me around the room, bumping into my back when I pivot towards my desk.

"I appreciate your predicament, but you should have

come to be first, Jared. I could have bought your stock. I have the money to buy you out, and I could have taken out a loan for Josh's shares. It would have stayed in the family. You didn't have to sell it to some godforsaken trust which may not have our best interest at heart." Dewy and over-heated, I slide my Chanel jacket from my arms and hurl it across my cluttered desk. It's not new and a little frayed on the edges, but it's a classic. Ever since I crunched the numbers and looked at our bottom line, I've had to curtail my expenses. It's a shame my brothers couldn't join me in the land of frugality. I have little doubt their spending habits and dwindling inheritance played a part in their treachery.

"Jana! No, you couldn't!" Macy chimes in unexpectedly. "You can't go into that kind of debt. Jared, don't let her go into that kind of debt!" She flies to her feet, spinning head-first into a whirlwind of hysterics. Macy Ramos is God's gift to the world of Finance. She's a phenom---a numbers freak who spent her college summers interning with the big dogs on Wall Street. Each one would hire her tomorrow, but she's holding out for the job and man of her dreams. I should have never mentioned the word debt in front of her. "Do something, Jared!"

Jared waves his arms across his chest like an umpire calling a time-out. "No fucking way, Jana. That's precisely why we didn't tell you. Dad left us this company, knowing damn well he was three billion in the hole and on the verge of being sued. And then he had the balls to look us in the face and ask us not to sell it---to cherish his legacy. We needed out yesterday. All of us." He paces to the door then turns to lean on it, crossing his arms over his chest. "We're selling this garbage."

"Don't talk to me about Dad's legacy. That's not why I'm holding on. There are three hundred people out there counting on me, on us, for their jobs. They don't get to cash in fifty million worth of stock and call it a fucking day!" My nerves catch up to my voice and turn my whisper into a screech. I slap my hand over my mouth, fearful someone outside might have heard.

Jared shakes his head once, exasperated with my naïveté. "If we don't bail. We'll inherit that fucking debt and might end up giving testimony before Congress. I can't help anyone but me." He steps closer, shuffling his feet like an adolescent boy seeking forgiveness. "I know you wanted to save it, and I love you for trying. If it wasn't sinking so fast, I'm sure you would've made it ten times better than Dad. But I'm begging you, stop wasting your time. It's not worth it. Talk to Mitchell Carnegie. He's offered to buy our stock."

My brain freezes then sputters aimlessly like a malfunctioning machine that needs to be reset. "Carnegie? You want to sell your shares to Carnegie?" I look at Macy, then Jared, and then back to Macy, choking on bile that's moments from making a gruesome appearance. This can't be true. He'll buy their stock for rock-bottom prices like a two-bit grifter, stiff them for the cash and then strip my company for parts. There is no way in hell I'll let that charlatan anywhere near this place. I don't care what I need to do.

I gaze stupefied at my brother and read his blank expression like a book. The truth sinks in before he can utter a word. "How far are you in this process, you imbecile?"

Jared feigns shock, mumbling as he inches towards the door, too ashamed to look me in the eye. "We've met with him once. We haven't closed anything yet."

"Don't you dare see him again. Carnegie doesn't have the funds to pay you anything. Macy will run his financials if you don't believe me. And if you're so desperate to sell, let me look for buyers, someone who can help the company with a merger or cash injection and not only line your pockets." I pace with fury, chewing my nails and wearing a path across my tiny Turkish rug, a gift from my mother.

Macy flies to my desk and goes to work on my laptop, clicking away while I rack my brain on possible allies. The only viable solution appears and reappears in my mind, but I push them away, fearing what their allegiance could cost me in the end.

"Janie, you've done enough. We'll deal with Carnegie." Jared tries to interrupt my strategic meeting for one, but I hold my hand up and silence him.

"No one has the kind of money to save this sinking ship." He steps closer and barks in my face. "At least, no one who will take a chance on us. Let it go. If Carnegie screws us over, then I guess we've got it coming. I'll have someone check him out before we give him our shares."

"The Valerians do." I stick my finger into his chest and bark back. "You don't know everything, Jared Penrose. The Valerians would offer you more money for your shares, and they could easily buy us out and possibly build something bigger. We may be sinking, but this ship has good bones. We're not a total loss." I turn to Macy, who appears just as stunned as my brother.

"Vladimir Valerian hated Dad. Why would he help us?" My brother won't admit he's intrigued, but I can clearly see the dollar signs floating around his head. He's willing to consider anything that might bring him a few extra bucks.

I nod and fold my arms across my chest. "Dad is gone. Vlad despised him for good reason, but he's never hated me. And his brothers have been trying to get into my sensible panties for the past year."

"Janie! They're like twice your age!" Jared clutches

imaginary pearls and sways in his Doc Martens. For heaven's sake, he really needs to revamp his wardrobe.

"Oh, shut up. Only Vlad is twice my age and not even. I'm a twenty-three-year-old woman running a corporation. I've got responsibilities. If I need to throw myself under the bus and sleep with one or two of the hottest men in the corporate world to save my employees from becoming destitute, then goddamn it, I shall." I turn to Macy, stick out my tongue then reach for my purse. "Besides, this is your fault. You've driven me to exchange sexual favors."

Spinning in his imaginary world of shame, Jared blocks my retreat. "I can't let you do this. You're not throwing yourself at three men to save this company."

My eyes grow wide with confusion. "Dummy, I'm kidding. Do I look like a prostitute? I'll meet with them to discuss a merger. Maybe I'll show a little leg to cut a better deal. Now, get out of my way before I find out one of them is gay and send you in wearing skinny jeans."

Chapter 2

Jana

"You can do this, Jana. I know you can. Do you know you can?" Macy spritzes perfume and shakes imaginary pompoms, fondly reliving her days as the head cheerleader of Exeter Academy. I smile to myself and remember her in her heyday. I watched from the sidelines as she kicked, bounced, cheered, and somersaulted her way into everyone's hearts, reciting every cheer in my head. As much as I wanted to join her, I never tried out. My father convinced me cheerleading was a self-indulgent waste of time and mocked me for considering it.

It's a silly thing, but it remains one of my biggest regrets.

"Yes, yes. My father will probably turn over in his grave the minute we shake hands, but I think I've moved past his feelings. I'm too busy cleaning up his mess to care." I step into my pumps and fasten the last button on my jacket, hoping to hide her ridiculous hot pink camisole that barely covers my nipples. I don't know how I allowed her to talk me into something so outrageous. This meeting may not even last more than five minutes.

"I thought you said you were going into that meeting

with both guns blazing?" She unfastens my button and lifts my boobs.

"Quit that! I meant my business guns. I didn't mean I'd shoot bullets out of my tits. Vlad's my old boss. I interned for him the summer between freshman and sophomore year. You don't flash your boobs to your old boss." I brush her hand away from my cleavage and button up.

"You don't?" Macy whips her head, horrified by this new information.

I roll my eyes and walk back my words, remembering her obsession with her former boss, Hunter King. "Sorry. That's not a rule. I mean, I'd feel awkward flirting with Vlad. I haven't seen him in years. He's a grown man pushing forty, and he's not into girls like me. I'm too young, and he's too cranky. It's like a female Elmo hooking up with Oscar the Grouch. Nobody wants to see that show. If Ilya and Maxim attend, I swear I'll make you proud." I check myself in the mirror and recall the last time I saw the Valerian twins.

This past Fourth of July weekend, Macy dragged me to a new club in Tribeca. She loves to dance, but it's never been my thing. I sat by the bar like a wallflower, nursing a frozen Margarita until Ilya and Max talked me into a dance. One dance turned to four, and I found myself sandwiched between two brothers, grinding, sweating, stealing kisses, and exchanging filthy fantasies for close to an hour. We talked about going back to their place, but of course, I chickened out.

I grit my teeth and sigh with regret. It's just one more thing to add to my what-if pile.

"Are we done?" I lift my wrist and take note of the time. My meeting with Vlad begins in forty-five minutes, and I'd like to arrive with only enough time to appear punctual, not early. I'm sure he's heard I'm desperate. I don't need to confirm his suspicions.

"Just one more thing." Macy rushes to my bureau, rummages through my jewelry box, and returns with a shiny gold crucifix. Without asking, she winds it around my neck and dangles it between my breasts. "This will draw his eyes to your cleavage, but because it's Jesus, you look totally innocent of any wrongdoing." She winks and subtly flicks open my top button, hoping I don't notice her sleight of hand.

"Please, stop that. I'm not practicing the art of seduction by thrusting my tits in his face. I'll only make a giant ass of myself." I know she means well, but I am aware of my limitations.

"Why are you so down on yourself? You're a beautiful girl. His brothers like you. I bet they have similar tastes." Macy is the queen of compliments. She hands them out so easily, it's hard to believe all of them are sincere.

"No." I button up.

Annoyed with my defiance, Macy throws her arms in the air and groans, "Jana Penrose, will you please stop hiding your assets and let that push-up bra work its magic. I have no doubt Vlad Valerian believes you're a competent businesswoman. You have nothing to prove, but you need his help. He hasn't seen you in years, and a man is a man. They all have a one-track mind. They can't help it. Plus, you said yourself, there is so much on the line."

"I'm not trying to be difficult, and I know how to play the game. I'm willing to smile, show some leg, drop a pen and take longer than average to pick it up. I do a hundred squats a day to maintain my ass, and I'll show it off for the sake of my employees. But this push-up bra is false advertising. It makes me look like a double D, and I'm a solid C."

Anxious to leave, I push her away and spin around in search of my bags.

"Quit being a baby." She fluffs my hair and nudges me towards the foyer, whispering in my ear like a tiny devil with her God-given ginormous boobs. "Hush up and listen. Since you can't plant your ass on his desk, you gotta work with what you have. Talk business with the man but gain the upper hand by sticking your boobs in his face. It'll make him forget his own name. I know what I'm talking about." She winks, then hands me my purse.

"You're insane," I mumble and reach for the door. "Leave your ringer on. I may need a ride from the police station after my tits fly out of this bra, and Valerian has me arrested for public nudity."

"He won't have you arrested. But he may marry you."

Chapter 3

Jana

"That's an incredible request, Miss Penrose. What's in it for me?" His gruff reply silences my well-rehearsed speech before I reach my thoughtful conclusion. Maybe Macy was right. I should have stunned him with my carefully constructed cleavage first. Why the hell am I so stubborn?

Perhaps I'm in over my head. Four years ago, I traipsed through these halls as a part-time intern, splitting my time between Maxim's Finance and Ilya's Marketing Departments. I was a nobody and rarely saw any of the Valerian brothers. Except on days when I wore miniskirts. Ilya always noticed me when I wore short skirts. But I digress.

It was my father's idea to set me up for an internship. He and Vlad were on better terms then, and the brothers welcomed me into their company with open arms. However, my father had different ideas. He wanted me to spy on his friend, gather information on a possible future competitor, and recruit any talent that appeared worth stealing. I did not comply with his wishes. The Valerians were kind and didn't deserve my treachery. Before I left, I told Vlad my father was about to double-cross him on a deal. I felt I owed him that much. He didn't automatically take my word, but my warning made him take the necessary precautions to learn the truth. He thanked me later, and my father never learned who betrayed him.

As we sit in silence, I consider leaving. I almost skipped out entirely. When Vlad's pinched face assistant led me through the executive wing of Quest Headquarters, the Valerian flagship corporation, I nearly bolted into the nearest stairwell. So, what made me change my mind? What the hell made me strut into Vladimir Valerian's office, one pump in front of the other, shoulders back, breasts thrust forward, shaking my ass like Jessica Rabbit? Sex.

One look into Vlad Valerian's smoldering blue eyes and four lonely years of sexual deprivation came crashing down at my feet. The last time I saw him, I was still knee-deep into my skinny, rock star bad boy phase and soundly unaware of how hot a well-built man of a certain age could be. I'm such a fool. Until today, I've never taken more than a passing glance at the man my father often called the devil incarnate.

And now that nickname only makes him sound hotter.

"Really?" I swallow the lump in my throat and let my fingers trail down the grooves of the gold crucifix nestled between my breasts. His eyes follow my hand, narrowing as they scrutinize their path into my cleavage. His smug expression fades as he leans forward and shamelessly ogles. I lean back and wiggle into my seat, just enough to jiggle my breasts. My feminist sensibilities die a horrible death and good riddance as far as I'm concerned. These are trying times, and my panties are wetter than the Atlantic.

I sink my teeth into my bottom lip and produce a genuine pout. "I apologize, Mr. Valerian. It was a mistake coming, and I've wasted enough of your time." I squirm forward, then dip down to grab my purse off the floor, giving him a generous view of my tits hoisted to their full potential thanks to my new push-up bra.

"Thank you for your time. It was lovely seeing you again. Please give my regards to Ilya and Max."

He quickly stands, extending his hand to halt my retreat. "Miss Penrose..." I give him an obligatory shake but pause when the touch of his warm skin makes my brain fizzle like an uncapped bottle. My pupils focus like robotic lasers, glued with perverse admiration to the masculine hands holding mine. They're stunning---too beautiful for mere mortals. They'd cover my breasts with ease.

"Miss Penrose?" he repeats himself.

"Yes?" I sway like a leaf in the wind, then gaze mesmerized at every glorious angle of his chiseled face. This is so unfair. Why are these men so pretty?

"Please, don't go. Not yet. I have other propositions to discuss." My eyebrow quirks when his heated gaze meets my stunned expression. "Other propositions?"

He nods once and gestures for me to retake my seat. "Please, allow me to explain." Remembering Macy's words, I shimmy my ass into the corner of his desk and cross my legs, frustrated I've lost my upper hand and trying like hell to win it back. It probably isn't even him, but the pull of the forbidden. He's sixteen years older than me and a bit of a daddy. Or maybe it's the fit of his suit: hand-tailored, perfect lines, snug on his chest, tight on his biceps, and an excellent little lift on his ass. There's so much more to him than those hands.

I really need to have sex. Soon. Very soon.

"Miss Penrose, may we end with these formalities? May I call you Jana?" He abandons his earlier scowl, and his mouth curves into a slight smile---nothing toothy, but just enough to set me at ease.

"Like I said, Vlad..." My teeth rake across my lips to pronounce the *vl* sound, and my heart skips a beat, tickled by the way it rolls off my tongue. "My concern is mainly for my employees. If I lose my shares and my stake in Penrose, I'll still have a comfortable life with my inheritance. It will be substantially less, but I can do with less. My employees will have nothing."

"Please, hear me out." He unbuttons his overcoat and slips his jacket off his arms, teasing me cruelly by thrusting the well-defined outline of his pectoral muscles directly into my face. The little jerk is paying me back.

I nod and unbutton my jacket, squirming to adjust my position. Vlad's eyes dance, following the bounce of my breasts as I straighten my posture and heave my chest into his line of sight. Two can play this game, mister.

"I'm listening," I purr, channeling my best sex kitten and oblivious to anything but the movement of his full lips and the sky-blue eyes peering deep into my soul. No wonder he's so successful. Those big eyes must shock his opponents into submission.

He clears his throat and shifts his gaze from side to side as if he's trying to recall words on the tip of his tongue. "Miss... I mean, Jana, I need to discuss this with my brothers."

"Of course. Perhaps we can follow up in a few days." I hop off his desk and straighten my skirt. I should have seen that coming. They're business partners and would need to discuss something this big. This isn't bad news.

"Jana Penrose, where the hell have you been hiding?" I startle and nearly stumble to the ground at the sound of Ilya Valerian's husky growl. My cheeks heat, and machine-gun giggles emerge as I cover my obscene cleavage with my purse. Ever since our close-call threesome, I've shamelessly ghosted him by changing my number and disappearing from all social media. Due to my cowardice, I've been forced to return to my ridiculous college email handle of bunnylover97.

"Hi!" I wave my fingers like a child and offer a toothless grin, reminiscent of that brief phase in primary school when I lacked the skills to smile.

"Hi?" He narrows his gaze in anger and storms towards me, teeth bared and breathing fire. "Is that all you have to say? Do you have any idea... oh fuck it..." He catches me by the waist, cradles me in his arms, and smashes his lips into mine. I lose my breath but find it in a kiss that carries me into the stars, past the moon, and drops me into cloud nine. Every swipe of his tongue leaves me spinning with desire and weak with lust. No one has ever kissed me like this. I'm pretty sure no one has ever tried.

Aware someone is watching, I push my fingers into his chest and thrill at the touch of the bulging muscles hidden from view. He lifts his dark gaze to mine, and the deep longing in his eyes leaves a tingling in the pit of my stomach. I don't understand what's happened. "How could you do that?" he whispers between kisses, but I'm too dazed to reply. "What does she need, Vlad? Whatever she needs, I'm in."

"Okay. That's one down." Vlad appears unaffected and makes no moves to curb his brother's strange behavior. Fortunately, Maxim arrives.

"Will you leave her alone?" Maxim approaches and whisks me out of his brother's grip. "I'm sorry, Jana. Ilya is incredibly overbearing." His velvet tenor and soft brown eyes bring me back to our night on the dance floor. The things he said---the things I said. Dear Lord, what if he remembers?

He offers me a seat and takes the one next to me, hovering close in a protective pose. Instead of taking the seat on the other side of Max, Ilya stands behind me, like an overprotective guard dog with no plans to let me out of his sight.

Vlad explains the situation with Penrose Media, the problem with my brothers selling their portion of the company, and my fear of mass layoffs if I lose control. Both Ilya and Maxim listen and agree to help me however they can. Neither put up a struggle nor ask too many questions over the hundreds of millions of dollars I'm asking them to put on the line.

My stomach flips, then flops. Something's wrong--- nothing happens this quickly in business. I know the Valerians have more money than God, but they have it because they're shrewd businessmen who don't just take any offer some chick with a push-up bra developed by NASA tosses their way. Maybe this is one big joke at my expense. Was Ilya's kiss part of it? Sweet Jesus, I'll never live this down.

"Jana, we have a lot of work ahead of us. We'll need to get started right away." Vlad's stern voice interrupts my downward spiral of dread.

"What?" The air leaves my lungs and strangles me into silence. He can't mean it. Not so soon. Not without more conditions.

"I won't do this alone, Jana. I don't have much interest in media, and frankly, I don't believe you have the experience to handle it all on your own. You'll have to hire the best people in the industry to help you. My brothers will help you play hardball, and I'll sign whatever checks you need.

But I want to see proposals and financials. Plus, your brothers are out, and I want you here full time."

"We should talk about this over dinner tonight." Ilya interjects, placing both his hands on my shoulders. "We'll be partners, now. We should act like partners."

"Partners?"

"It's too soon for that, Ilya. You're getting way ahead of yourself." Vlad's voice softens as he steps around his desk and attempts to put Ilya in his place. My confusion deepens. Am I a partner?

"Miss Penrose, you don't need to go to dinner with three men. Ilya's intentions are hardly innocent. But I don't need to tell you that. Yes, you would be our partner in this venture since you bring a small part of your shares. We're not equal partners, but your expertise counts for plenty. I will ensure you are well compensated. We can go over details next week."

With Maxim's help, I stand to leave. I don't feel his hands grip my waist until he pulls me into his arms. I can't feel my feet leave the ground until he places me on his powerful thighs and holds me close. I should feel stunned, accosted, violated by a strange man, but I don't. Cooing gently, he wraps me in his warm embrace and assures me I'll be fine. It isn't sexual. It's affectionate. Maxim brushes the hair off my collar and whispers in my ear, "We missed you, Jana. Come out with us tonight. I would never let you do anything you didn't want to do."

I hum something in the affirmative and cling to his lapels, nuzzling my face against his hard pecs. I'm too lost in the scent of his cologne to argue with a man who smells this good. "What time?"

"We'll pick you up at 8:oo." Ilya yanks me out of

Maxim's lap and brings his lips to my forehead. "We won't rush you into anything. We'll go at your speed."

"My speed?" I stammer and lift my wide eyes to his, finally aware that we may not be talking about the state of Penrose Media anymore.

He nods and brings my hand to his lips. "Of course, it will always be about you."

Chapter 4

Vlad

"**A**re you okay?" My brother, Max, tugs my sleeve, clearing his throat multiple times to draw my attention to him.

"What? No. Yes, I don't know." I thread my hand through my sweat-soaked hair and continue to stare at the hypnotic sway of Jana Penrose's luscious hips. When she disappears into an adjoining hall, she releases me from her cruel spell and uncurls her talons from my icy heart. I stand listless, confused by the ache in my soul and the stiff cock taking up far too much space in my pants. I'm sure this has never happened before.

"You like her, don't you?" When a small group of curious employees gathers close, Max nudges me into my office, blocking everyone's view of his crazy catatonic brother, and waves them back to work.

"I'm...fine." I stutter and stumble through the door frame, struggling to regain my senses. My hazy mind reflects on the last half hour and the strange turn of events that unfolded. The last time I laid eyes on Cecil Penrose's daughter, she was a waifish little thing who betrayed her father to do the right thing. I agreed to see her today because I respect that kind of honesty in people and because my brothers insisted. I didn't think I'd gaze into her angelic face, supple curves, and kissable lips then lose my fucking nerve to stand firmly against whatever she had to say.

When she walked into my office, I swore she stepped out of a dream. One look from those dark eyes awakened a part of my heart I was sure didn't exist. A few words from those full red lips and my restless soul calmed. I never believed in soul mates. I never dreamt of searching for my other half until she walked into my office and asked for my help. It took every ounce of strength not to give in to her every demand.

Ilya was right. She gets under your skin without even trying.

"Vlad?" Max interrupts my mindless rambling and follows me to my desk. He's unaccustomed to this side of me. I'm almost sure he saw me hanging on every word Jana spoke while we said our goodbyes.

I nod, mouth slacked, eyes glued to the door, hoping against hope that she might appear at my threshold, having left something behind. "Where are we going to dinner?"

"Ilya made reservations at Gianni Russo's." He spits it out and waits for me to comment, almost certain I'll have something to say about the location. And he's correct.

"Is he out of his mind? Absolutely not." I fly out of my chair and walk back to the door, searching the hall for that idiot's smug, impatient face. There's nothing seedy about Gianni Russo's. It's one of the nicest Italian restaurants in Brooklyn. But Club Sin is less than two blocks away. Only patrons know it's there, and I'm almost sure she's not a member. The cringeworthy thought leaves a bad taste in my hypocritical mouth. I can't picture my lovely girl in a place like that---not without us. But that isn't the point. He's chosen that place because he hopes to take her there.

"I think he's playing with fire too, but he swears she was close in July, and he doesn't want to wait. He's in love with her. Ilya hasn't been with another woman since last year--- not since he fell for Jana. I mean, neither have I, but I was never as much of a hound dog in the first place.

"This could go horribly wrong, Max." I clench my fist and punch it into my palm. "If she is the one and we move too fast, we could ruin everything."

Max walks to the door, chuckles, and turns to face me. "Let's not overthink this. Jana's different. She's used to dealing with men. She walked into scary Vlad Valerian's office to fight for her employees when she knew there was a good chance you'd say no. Let her tell us what she wants, and then all we have to do is give it to her."

"Just like that?" I smirk at his simple answer.

"Yep. Just like that. I'm in love with that girl. I'm willing to wait, but if I can have her tonight, fuck it, I'll dive into the fucking deep end and pull her under. See you tonight, big brother."

Chapter 5

Jana

I've spent my whole life swallowing my emotions because my father considered them a sign of weakness. My gender didn't matter. He raised me like my brothers and told me to be as tough as nails. I had to put my needs aside and do what was best for the family. But that was bullshit. As far as he was concerned, he was the family, and my life revolved around pleasing him.

Macy was right. It feels good to be a girl. It felt good being sexually objectified by three men I wanted to strip naked and ride bareback into the New York sunset. Sweet Jesus, how will I ever make it through dinner without asking for sex from one or two---dare I say, three men? No, who has sex with three men?

Is that a thing? Is it? I mean outside pornography because I'm not setting those kinds of goals. I need to look this up on the internet.

One foot in front of the other. It's such a simple act. I've been doing it since infancy, but it's never easy when three of the hottest men you've ever met are watching you walk away. There is no sense looking over my shoulder to verify their presence. I can feel their eyes glued to my ass.

Come on, Jana, don't force it, and please don't fall back into your typical waddle. Eyes forward, shoulders back, relax your hands, and swing your arms slightly---not too much for heaven's sake. Put on a show but don't give away the farm. Make them work for it but let them know you're open for business. Business? For crying out loud, that's not the word I want to be associated with right now.

I'm not imagining it. I'm naïve, but I'm not that obtuse. Those twins want to pick up where we left off. Dinner is the opening act for a threesome. I know I said I needed sex, but can I handle two men at once? Does Vlad plan on watching? What's the point in that? The man is drop-dead gorgeous. If he's in the room, why wouldn't he service me too?

I can't believe my own ears. And I can't believe I have nothing to wear to my very own foursome. Everyone's already seen my one sexy brassiere. Everything else I own is white and functional. I better call Macy. If I text, she'll think I've been kidnapped and using code to tip her off.

Perhaps I'm jumping the gun. I don't know anything about swingers and poly sex. This is a huge gamble. I just really hope I don't spend a ton of money on new underwear for nothing.

Chapter 6

Ilya

"I don't think you've spent enough time thinking about what pleases you, Jana. And I want to know all about what pleases you." I stare into the murky depths of her dark eyes and wonder how long it would take to lose myself in the bottomless pools. This girl is long overdue for a proper release. And I don't mean a simple climax--- she'll soon tire of those. If she lets us into her life, her next climax will always be just around the corner.

I mean a true release. To experience something like that, she needs to let go of all her inhibitions. Right now, that's all I see.

She fights the urge to smile, then ducks her head, fidgeting with the napkin in her lap as she tries to think of a proper reply. "What do you mean? I'm pleased with the direction you'll take Penrose, I mean Valiant. I like that name. Vlad has a much clearer vision than my father." She lifts her wine glass towards Vlad then brings it to her lips. Maxim smirks. He knows me well. As much as I want her to fall in love with both my brothers---right now, I want her eyes on me.

"It will please me tremendously if you maintain fifty percent of my staff and provide a decent severance for the others. But I suppose we can speak more about that next week. This place is lovely. Who chose it?" She flutters her lashes then shifts her gaze from me to Maxim, then Vlad.

"Ilya chose it," Vlad calls me out before I can answer. He thinks this was a bad idea, but I have no doubt he'll join us at Club Sin if she agrees.

I extend my arm to her side of the table and offer my hand. She hesitates for a moment, then walks her fingers into my palm, giggling when I snare her hand in my bear trap. Her gaze catches mine, and her brown eyes glimmer in the candlelight. She's so fucking beautiful. My heart swells and squeezes the air from my lungs. "I don't mean professionally. We'll take care of your people, Jana. I want to know about you. Do you want to stay in media?"

Her expression stills then mingles with a hint of curiosity. She doesn't understand why I want to know such a peculiar thing, but she wants to answer. "When this is settled and running on its own, I'd like to run something smaller. I'd like something I can manage from a small home office in case I start a family---if that day ever comes. My father used to think it was silly." She shrugs, and the luster that sparkled all around her moments ago fades.

"The hell with your father, Jana. I don't think it's silly at all." I give her a wink and delight when a pink flush blooms on her cheeks.

"No doubt you'll excel at motherhood" Her round eyes flash to mine, then quickly move about the table, hoping to latch on to something other than my eager expression.

"You're teasing me. But there's no rush when you want to do things right." She's stunning and utterly oblivious to how much her life is about to change. We'll give her whatever she wants, whenever she wants it. If not us, then me alone.

This afternoon, I wasn't myself. This emotion is so utterly foreign I was convinced it was nothing more than a temporary obsession brought on by a pair of dark eyes, luscious breasts, and months of sexual deprivation. After Jana left, I spent the following hours talking myself off the ledge. Now, I'm sure I've lost my heart. And I know she's the one.

My brothers and I rarely speak of the details. It's just understood we'll build our lives together. It's something we rant about when we're drunk or looking for someone at Club Sin. But truth be told, we've never tested the waters. Until now, we've only dabbled with sharing a woman when our hearts weren't on the line.

Jana isn't like the other women. She could recoil with disgust at the mere suggestion of three men devouring her sumptuous body like a Thanksgiving buffet. I need to stop this. This is no time to get an erection. Not another one.

"Is everything okay?" Jana's sweet voice reminds me we're having dinner, and too much time has passed without a word between us. There's so much to say, but my lust-addled brain refuses to send the proper signals. Compliments, pleasantries, and words of admiration clog my throat and leave me lovestruck.

My face heats under her gaze. Surely, I'll incinerate into a pile of ash and never have to relive this humiliation again. But then I'd never get to sink my bare cock into her wet sex over and over, harder and faster, until she screams for me to make her my good girl. Jesus Christ, I can't wait. I scratch the palm of my hand with my fingers, itching like crazy to feel it slap against the supple skin of her voluptuous ass.

"No, it's not." I make a bold move and slide closer. Her

body tenses, but she makes no attempt to flee. It's a small victory, but I take the win. I reach between her inner thighs and part her legs, searching her eyes for any signs of protest. There aren't any.

"Jana..." Our eyes lock in a heated gaze that sends her straight into my arms. My control plummets. The taste of her kiss makes me lose my mind and launches my hand into her panties. She lifts one leg over my thigh and grants me access to my overwhelming relief and endless gratitude.

We need to leave. I need to tell her where we should go. But she's so wet, and the tablecloth is long enough to shield our naughty activity below the waist. "Ilya," she purrs when my fingers find her hard button, then surprises me by placing her hand over my cock.

I groan into her lips and deepen our kiss, wishing she'd tighten her grip around my shaft and take me into her mouth. But that's not the way I want this to go. We'll start this right and have her together.

I take her wrist in my hand, smile, and pull it off my crotch. "Not yet, sweetheart. There's somewhere we should go."

"Somewhere?" Her lips part then spread into a slight smile. She's intrigued and maybe a little titillated. Jana looks to Vlad, then Max, both stunned and sweaty with eyes as wide as saucers, then brings those big brown eyes back to me. "Should we go now?"

My heart explodes, but for the sake of keeping the façade of control, I nod and lift my hand for the check. "We should go now."

Chapter 7

Maxim

This is never an easy conversation. Ilya's in love, and he wants what he wants when he wants it. But the object of our affection has never spent time in our world. If you can call it our world. We've never lived a polyamorous life---not yet. The women we've met at Club Sin were sexual distractions at best. Jana's different. If we take her there, we'll take her home. And we've never taken anyone home.

"You brought me here for a reason." Jana walks ahead of us. Her confident gait and saucy strut return as she lifts her arms overhead, stretching like a kitten after a nap, then turns to face our curious expressions. Her long brown locks blow wildly in the cool autumn breeze as she waits for one of us to answer her question.

I step forward and stare bewildered, unsure how to answer a question that wasn't asked. "Here?"

She nods and attaches one hand to her hip. "Do you want to know why my father left me in charge of his company?"

I shake my head, expecting to hear something about her

intelligence and business prowess. I've followed her career since she worked for us four years ago. She's a force of nature, and although she's young, she's got incredible instincts. There's so much more to her than beauty.

Her wide eyes narrow into slits as the corners of her mouth twist with exasperation. "He didn't think I was fit to lead. He didn't think anyone could replace him. My father chose me over my brothers because he thought I would be easy to control after he retired. But I'm not. I saw through his head games from the beginning. Are you three faking this crazy infatuation to control me?"

Our jaws hit the pavement. Ilya, Vlad, and I gasp like a trio of church ladies at Sunday service. Pushing each other off, we try to reach her to explain our intentions, but she lifts her hand and holds us off.

"Listen, I won't put up with cruel jokes. In twenty-three years, I've had one boyfriend. So, it feels a little strange that three men appear out from the ether and want me so badly they're willing to share." She spins on her heels like a petulant brat and gives us her back.

I jump forward and try to explain the unexplainable. "I know it feels strange, but we've always been close. We always fall for the same woman. That's how it is with us. Except we've never felt anything like this before. And I think you feel it too. "

"And what's Club Sin?" She peeks at me from beneath her lashes and stammers, "The woman in the restroom called it a sex club."

"That's where we want to take you. If you'd like to go." I take her hand in mine and lift it to my lips. "Or we can take you home. The choice is yours."

"Are you swingers?" She mumbles, then looks past me

to Vlad and Ilya, who shake their heads and turn beet red at the implication.

Vlad flies forward and whisks Jana out of my arms, taking control of the conversation and quickly setting her mind at ease. "No swinging. No other women. Let's go have a look, and if you hate it, we'll leave and grab a drink somewhere else. This is all about you, Jana. We want to know what pleases you."

Chapter 8

Jana

I grew up with boys. When you have two brothers who demand as much attention as mine, you learn to fight for every flicker of spotlight you can garner. I let my father shape me into something I wasn't, into something that never fit, because I didn't want to be invisible anymore. But the older I got, the more I found boys will always be boys. No matter how much I tried to play with the big boys, there would always be those who just picked up their ball and went home.

Today, I figured out, I don't need to play their game anymore. This afternoon, I got precisely what I wanted by doing exactly what I wanted to do. And who knows what tonight may bring.

Outside, the place looks like nothing more than a subdued luxury hotel that blends into the background. If you don't know what you're looking for, you might miss it. There are no glaring signs that say Club Sin. No sounds of whips being cracked. I see no scantily-clad mistresses handing out condoms or ball-gagged submissives on all fours being led like beasts of burden. I'm not sure what I expected when I entered the dark-walled, dimly-lit foyer of the only sex club I've ever visited.

"Are you nervous?" Vlad whispers, clutching my hand tightly to his as he leads us into one of the many lounges in the center of the club. It isn't only a place where people come to hook up. Maxim tells me monogamous couples rent specialized rooms that cater to their predilections. There are bondage rooms, orgy rooms, and rooms designed to better serve polyamorous couples who need unique furniture. I stumble in my pumps, shocked by his words and stunned by the amount of moisture pooling in my panties.

I give him a weak smile and shake my head. Of course, I'm nervous. It's three penises against one. That's hardly a fair fight.

When we reach a high-top table, Vlad orders a bottle of champagne, and Ilya slides in behind me. He winds his arm around my waist and pulls me into his chest, reclaiming his place by my side. "We can stay here, and people watch, kitten. We don't have to go to a room." He rests his chin on the top of my head and sighs, perhaps remorseful he may have rushed me into something before I'm ready.

I don't answer. Not yet. It's not a matter of being ready. Are you ever prepared for your first time with three men? I'm just thinking about positions, logistics, leg placement, and the fact that three men will see me completely nude when the last time I refused to remove my sports bra. Truth be told, I'm not sure I'm a good lover. When it's one on one, you can blame the other person. But if it's four people and you're the only woman, it might become apparent you're the problem.

What if we go into that room, and I crash and burn? What if no one has an orgasm? I will die on the spot.

Maxim hands me a flute of champagne with two raspberries floating in the center. I lift my eyes to his, and my belly winds into a tight coil of anticipation. I'm doing this. Jana Penrose is taking it up a notch. No more what-ifs. No looking back on my life with a long list of regrets. Three gorgeous men want to take me into a private room for one night of raunchy sex. How can I say no? I've been so good for so long, and this year has sucked so hard. A three penis night just might make up for it.

"I don't want to be me." I make my announcement to the table and arouse three looks of confusion. Ilya quirks an eyebrow. Maxim cocks his head. Vlad leans closer and demands to know more.

"What does that mean?" Vlad's stern voice returns, and the deep vibration so close to my ear sends a nasty tingle down my spine. I think I'll start with him. No doubt, Ilya assumes he'll go first, but they keep repeating this is about me. And between the three, no one has my number more than Vlad.

"Try to understand, little girls aren't normally raised to embrace their sexuality. If and when we jump that hurdle, there's nothing in society that tells us we're allowed to fully enjoy three men at once. My libido needs to reconcile this with my brain, and for me to do that, I need to walk into the room, pretending I'm someone else. Does that make sense? Can we role play?" I take a sip of champagne to wet my whistle, having concluded my lesson in female sexuality.

They nod and slap their foreheads, sighing with relief and chuckling at their stupidity. "Of course, sweetheart. That sounds like an excellent idea." Vlad sidles close, and I curl into his chest, clutching his lapels to hide my face. "Who would you like to be?"

I take a deep breath and steel my nerves. "Anything? And you'll play along?"

"Are we aliens?" He smiles from ear to ear then bends down to kiss my forehead.

"You and I are married." My voice shakes as the words squeak out from my clenched throat. Vlad's thoughtful gaze begs me to continue. "Gentleman's choice. You take me first while they watch, or you offer me to your friends while you watch. I want it dirty, nasty---but no degradation."

He fights a smile. "I would never degrade you. But can I spank you?"

I nod. "Only my ass. Not on my breasts, legs, or feet. And nothing on my face."

"Never." His brow furrows deep, horrified that I'd think such a thing.

"I just need to be clear." I take another sip, then turn to Max and Ilya. "I don't know how much I can handle. I've only ever been with one man, and my experience is limited."

"Understood. If you want things to end, just say the word, red." Vlad lifts me off my stool and plants me on my feet. I stare up at his impressive height and drink him in like a tall drink of water on a scorching summer day. In minutes, I'll feel his hard body pressed against mine and feel his stiff cock slide deep inside me. Followed by two more. Sweet Jesus, what am I doing?

Hoping to regain control of my unbridled emotions, I make a second announcement. "And this is just for tonight. What happens here---stays here, just like Vegas. Monday, we begin as co-workers. Strictly colleagues, okay?" I look to each one and wait for a sign of agreement. Nothing greets me but confusion.

"No one's agreeing to that, Jana." Ilya twirls me under his arm and dips me. "Let's get a room before I bend you over a chair and take you here."

Chapter 9

Vlad

Ilya chooses Room Four. We've never used it before, but he claims he saved it for a special occasion. There's nothing extraordinary about it, but it is a room uniquely set up for four people. For obvious reasons, four is meant to be our lucky number. Since I'm not a superstitious man, I'll take his word for it.

From the moment we get our key, Jana plays her part. With nervous anticipation, she takes my hand, threading her fingers in mine and sealing her body against me as we walk hand in hand down the long red corridor of rooms. Maxim and Ilya's slow, heavy footsteps echo behind us, like two serial killers stalking their prey. Anything can happen. She could walk in, walk out and never speak to us again. The ball is entirely in Jana's court.

And oh boy, does Jana know how to play.

Jana steps in first, touring the room like a newlywed inspects the honeymoon suite on her wedding night. She examines the circular bed, tests the mattress's firmness, and then tiptoes towards the arched leather chaise specially made for easy access during double penetration.

I'll explain that to her later---or perhaps show her. The night is young.

Ilya and Maxim find two leather captain's chairs in the corner of the room and push them closer to the bed. If they're going to watch, they want a better view.

I peel off my jacket and hang it on a hook, anxious to begin but searching for the right words to put her at ease. I have particular preferences that I don't typically share in front of my brothers. When we come here, there isn't enough time to cultivate that kind of relationship with our partner for the evening. But Jana is for keeps. If I'm going to do this right, I need to start right from the beginning.

I unbuckle my belt, and the sound of clicking metal brings Jana rushing to my side. Her dark eyes, deep and wicked with mystery, stare into my heart and read me like an open book. "Let me do that, Daddy."

My eyes widen with shock, and my heart beats clean out of my chest. I take her face in my hands and seal my lips to hers. Our tongues slowly entwine in a sweltering kiss that sears this moment in my mind forever. While we kiss, her fingers work fast to unfasten my belt and yank it off my trousers. It's too soon to take out my dick. Once that happens, I'll want to put it inside her, and we'll reach the end of round one. I need to draw this out for the sake of her game.

I reach for her wrist and pull it off before she can unzip my pants. "Daddy wants to see what his little girl looks like under this dress." I walk her to the center of the room and watch her from the bed. "Will you undress for me? And my friends?"

She feigns innocence and smiles. A crimson blush stains her cheeks as she steps out of her shoes and gives us her back. "Can someone unzip me?"

Maxim jumps to his feet, pushing Ilya back into his chair, and obliges without question. He takes his time, letting his fingers trace her skin along the path of the zipper before helping her peel it off her shoulders.

"Thank you." Jana holds the crumpled silk in her hands then lets it fall to the floor.

Allowing Jana Penrose to stand before us in next to nothing is probably a massive miscalculation on my part. She's too beautiful for words and too stunning to take in all at once. My brain freezes, locked in admiration and stuck in a temporary state of madness. Ilya's jaw hangs open, and his mouth waters with hunger and avarice. Maxim appears to be struck blind from staring directly at the sun.

I can't believe she's ours. She may not understand it yet, but she will. There's no going back from here.

"Daddy?" While Jana waits for further instruction, she unhooks her bra and flings it at my face.

"Daddy's going to make his little girl pay for that." The sight of Jana's perfect breasts, the same ones she thrust in my face this afternoon, brings my simmering lust to a raging boil and unleashes the beast. I tackle her like a linebacker, fling her over my shoulder and toss her onto the bed. She lands with a bounce and hops up to unbutton my shirt.

"I'm sorry, Daddy. Did I do something wrong?" She brings her lips to mine, and I devour her mouth, suckling, and licking, mining for her taste like my life depends on it. I rip off her panties and toss them to my brothers. Ilya catches them mid-air and brings them to his face, inhaling the scent of her pussy and wishing he was me.

"You did. You teased me. Don't ever tease your Daddy, baby." I spread her legs and run my hand between her thighs, then kiss my way through her dripping core. She's soaking wet. The scent of her arousal hits my nostrils and makes my mouth water like a hot dish of fine cuisine. I drag my tongue through her slit and growl with hunger.

"Daddy?" Her soft whimper makes me smile, but I want to hear her scream.

"Daddy's going to fuck his little girl in front of his friends. That makes you hot. Doesn't it?" I bury my face in her glistening pussy and thrash her hard bud, lashing and striking it until her sweet cries fill the room and her sweet honey coats my beard.

Her legs tremble and bounce off the mattress. "Yes! I love it when Daddy's friends watch him fuck his little girl." The blush on her chest deepens and spreads to her limbs. Her breath catches and comes in pants. She moans profanities and mumbles nonsense, rocking her hips into my face so hard she nearly knocks me unconscious.

"Are you going to be a good girl and let Daddy's friends fuck you too?" I shove two fingers inside her pussy and pump them into her inner wall. She lifts her knees and points her toes, twisting in a fit of ecstasy that makes the twins scatter to the side of the bed, stroking their dicks without mercy.

She shakes violently, nodding her head and pulling the sheets as her body succumbs to the wildest orgasm I've ever witnessed. I cover her body with mine and growl against her tight nipples, swirling my tongue over each tight bud. "Your Daddy wants you so bad, baby."

"Fuck me, Daddy. Fuck your little girl." Jana runs her hands through my hair and presses my face to her breasts. If her nasty words weren't enough, the scent of her skin sends me into action.

I clasp her wrists and hold them over her head. With my free hand, I run the head of my cock through her wet slit, bumping her clit, once, twice, three times, until she moans and begs for my cock. I thrust into her tight pussy on the fourth pass, stretch her walls and fill her to the hilt. Inch after inch, she makes room for me, gasping with delight as she strangles my cock and nearly pushes me out. She can't get rid of me so fast. This pussy is too fucking good to lose my place. I come back for more and more, and we set a brutal pace that fills the room with the sounds of sex.

Maxim and Ilya watch, ready to join us, and as much as I'm enjoying the moment, it's unfair to keep her all to myself.

"Maybe you should be nicer to Daddy's friends." I flip her over and prop her up to her knees. With her gorgeous ass in view, I give her a good swat and repeat my instructions. "Why don't you take Ilya and Max in your mouth, baby."

She nods and curls her finger towards Maxim. Ilya doesn't need a prompt. He slides in next to him and waits his turn. While I take her from behind, thrusting and rutting her tight pussy, Jana takes Maxim's shaft into her warm mouth. She hums around his length, plunging up and down, taking him as far as she can while Ilya holds her hair. His hungry lovesick eyes take in every second, lost in admiration and eager to feel her lips wrapped lovingly around him.

She takes a breath and fists Ilya's cock, gasping at the sight of his thick member. He's the biggest and thickest of us all. But his size doesn't stop her. On the contrary, it seems to turn her on. She looks over her shoulder to me, then takes him as far as she can, gagging on his length and choking on his girth. He holds her head, nudging her down, then pulling her up again and again. She tosses her head back, and he bends down, covering her mouth in a fiery kiss as they exchange words of love. He wants his turn, and he's about to get it.

"Fuck, Jana." Her pussy clenches around my shaft, and my resolve weakens. With every thrust, my balls ache for release. Ramming harder and faster, I feel her shatter in my arms, trembling into spastic jerks that milk my cock and fill her pussy with hot cum.

This is just the beginning.

Chapter 10

Jana

My body craves the touch of six masculine hands exploring, claiming, demanding my submission, and wrecking my sex with every thrust. They're all I see. I inhale their scent with every breath and feel their voices vibrate through my skin. Whatever they want, I give freely. I scream my devotion with every plunge in every orifice because I'm no longer complete until I'm filled to the hilt and stuffed with Valerian cock.

For the second or perhaps third time, Ilya carries me to the chaise on the far side of the room. He gently licks my swollen lips, bruised from kissing three men for hours, and folds me into his lap. His hands caress my breasts, massaging my nipples as his mouth travels the length of my neck.

"Do you want to try it, kitten?" He purrs, nibbling into my shoulder, tempting me with certain damnation like the devil. Apart from oral play, I've only taken them one at a time, but we've been slowly working toward the ultimate undertaking for a woman pleasuring three men at once. I didn't walk into Room Four believing this would turn into my life. Tonight was supposed to be a one-and-done. But three hours in, and I'm not sure I could ever go back to one man. This next act could seal my fate or prove my ultimate undoing.

I lean back into his chest and spread my thighs to straddle his lap. "Can we take it slow?" I've hardly spoken the words when I feel Ilya's lubed cock gently snake its way into my ass. He's bigger than his brothers and the hardest to take. But goddamn, he makes me come hard and fast once he works his way into an easy rhythm. I dig my fingers into his muscular thighs and brace myself for the rest of his invasion, trembling as he creeps deeper and roots himself as far as he'll go.

"Ilya..." My breath hitches and a quiet gasp floats free as he penetrates my pussy with three fingers. "Ilya...oh, no..." I squeal through every thrust, but my protests have nothing to do with pain. He knows what he's doing. This is the third time we've had anal sex, and he already knows the precise angle I need to dissolve like a blubbering banshee.

"Give it to me, kitten," Ilya demands my climax, and without hesitation, I hand it over in a shattering fit that makes me fear I'll have to scream for the paramedics. He's magnificent and could be the death of me outside these four walls.

I fall back into his chest and close my eyes for no more than a second when I feel Maxim approach with his stiff cock in his hand. I'm not sure if it's the afterglow or Max's sweet face, but I welcome him into my embrace and help him slide his thick cock into my still quivering pussy.

"Oh, fuck..." There are no other words to describe the unbelievable feeling of two massive cocks filling me at once. Max hooks his elbows under my knees and roots himself deeper. Ilya cups his hands under my ass and adjusts our angle, working in tandem with his twin to ease me into each shaft, in and out, out then in, moving as one as they conquer me together. The scent of our skin, sweat, and arousal inflamed by our heat, blends together as the friction between us grows to a fevered pitch.

"Are you okay, sweetheart?" Maxim's lips find mine in a tantalizing kiss that gets me hotter, if that's possible. Anything's possible. I'm in a private room inside a sex club in Brooklyn with the three hottest men I've ever met. I'll surely learn this was all a nasty dream in the morning.

I nod and squeak, "Yes. Keep going. Where's Vlad?" I cry out his name without thinking, forever horny for my Daddy, who I spot watching us from across the room.

Vlad approaches, naked and hard, but makes no move to join in. He offers a warm, almost paternal smile and brushes the sweaty hair off my forehead while his younger brothers have their way with my body.

In a sick twist, that gets me hotter than the fucking Sahara.

"Daddy, please..." On the edge of release, teetering between a series of little deaths, I shamelessly plead for his cock. And he obliges. I take Vladimir into my mouth, with Ilya stuffed in my ass and Maxim thrusting deep in my pussy. Hot sex becomes a frenzy of epic proportions. The four of us, tied together, bound in one seamless juggernaut of primal lust, unites us in more ways than any of us understand. When I come, they come, and once again, each one marks me as theirs. It'll take me days to wash off their scent.

As we lie together, exhausted and silent, I feel nothing but the promise of things yet to come. Things I'm not sure I can handle.

Chapter 11

Jana

"**Y**ou're a real hussy. You know that?" I shove my sheets into the washer, toss a detergent tablet into the drum, and turn the setting to whites. The boys left thirty minutes ago. They didn't want to go, but after thirty-six hours, I needed time to recover, hydrate, stretch---I don't know what other women do in these situations. I'm new to the ways of the tramp, but if these are the rewards, I may be ready to embrace her lifestyle.

We spent most of the weekend making love. No, it wasn't love. They don't love me if they're willing to share me with one another---right? It was smoking hot sex in every position known to man. If I didn't need it so badly, I might have been able to resist their charms. And if I didn't have a long-dormant Daddy kink that needed purging, I wouldn't have jumped at the chance to have sex with Vlad. Which got me hooked on Ilya and Maxim. Dear Lord, I've fallen faster than Lucifer.

I tap the button on the washer and listen for the water. Once I'm satisfied the suds have begun removing the evidence of three men's passion, I dash into my bedroom and finish dressing. I've called an emergency meeting with my best friends, Macy and Willow, at our favorite coffee shop. Macy has been on call since Friday and was prepared for my all-points bulletin this morning. But Willow needed a tad more convincing. Once Macy spilled the beans about my first sexual encounter since those two lackluster months I spent as Jeremy Haven's sexually discontented girlfriend sophomore year in college, she flew out of bed.

As much as I love Macy's advice, I need Willow's experience at a time like this. Macy has a one-track mind. She's been in love with the same man since she was sixteen years old, a man old enough to be her father, and never deviated once. He can ignore her, look past her, and reject her advances when we all know he caught the Macy bug years ago. That girl won't give up until she breaks him because she's one hundred percent certain there's only one man for her.

Willow doesn't see the world in black and white. She knows there are shades of gray, and right now, I'm swimming in a great big pool of gray. I don't know up from down, right from left, or love from lust. This weekend didn't feel like a two-night stand. They made plans for Monday, Wednesday, and the weekend. Nothing makes sense, and yet nothing feels wrong. This should feel wrong. Why doesn't it feel wrong?

"No, it should definitely feel wrong." Macy squeezes the honey bear over her cup of peppermint tea and stirs it in, clinking the ceramic sides with a touch of judgment.

"Stop that." Willow grabs Macy's hand and holds it still. "That's the most annoying sound when you're nursing a hangover." She places her teaspoon on a napkin and turns to me. "Don't listen to Macy. If it doesn't feel wrong, then you kind of have your answer, Jana. You're not a sociopath.

You're one of the kindest women I know. If I were you, I would have sold those stocks weeks ago and been sunning myself on a beach in Bermuda right now. I wouldn't have given one thought to all the people losing their jobs. And not because I don't care. I'm just a self-absorbed jerk. All that business shit would have gone over my head until it was too late. But you put yourself out there. Stop being so down on yourself. And ignore Macy. Virgins don't get an opinion on our sexual misadventures until they have stories to contribute."

I shrink in my seat and slurp my hot chocolate, visualizing the length of Ilya's cock, Maxim's oral talents, and Vlad's skills getting me off. Where does Ilya hide something like that all day? How did Max get so good? I wonder what Vlad's doing right now.

"Are you ignoring me or remembering something nasty?" Macy's shrill interrupts my daydream and drags me back to reality.

"I remembered something nasty." I sit up straight and take another sip of chocolate, holding my pinky out to demonstrate I haven't lost my class.

She clears her throat and repeats the question I missed, "You know I love you, and I don't mean to call you names in any way, shape, or form. You're a grown woman who can do as she pleases. But I worry. You have a big heart, and I don't want you to get hurt. You don't strike me as the type who can have sex without any emotional attachment, and I find it hard to believe any man would form an attachment to you if he's perfectly okay with you sleeping with both of his brothers. Whether or not he's present. Say what you will, Willow, but you know it's true!" Macy gives us one big nod and defiantly folds her arms across her chest.

Willow and I stare at one another at a loss for words.

I've got no rebuttal that makes sense in Macy's strait-laced world or mine, for that matter. What kind of man shares you with his brothers? What kind of man indeed? They say this is who they are, but what the hell does that mean?

"Listen." Willow leans into the table and prepares to impart her particular brand of wisdom. Technically, she's not much more experienced than I was before this weekend, but she works in public relations and spends more than the average amount of time around celebrities. She insists they're way freakier than ordinary people. "Not everyone loves the same, Miss Ramos. If the Valerians plan to see Jana again on multiple occasions, they're obviously not looking to blow her off. Plus, they'll be working together. She starts on Monday. That doesn't sound like guys who plan to keep her at arm's length." She takes a sip of coffee and scoots her chair closer.

Macy won't be outdone. "You don't know how they'll treat her at work, Willow. Things might be different now that they've had their fun. I've known Jana since second grade, and I'm sorry if this strange scenario worries me."

"They don't seem like the type of men to play games. The Valerian brothers are close, and from what you describe, they want a polyamorous life with one woman. "Willow cocks her head and takes a sip of coffee. "Do you want to be that woman, Jana? Can you handle three husbands?"

I stare, confused, then look left to right. My panicked voice appears. "What? Three husbands? That's not legal." I hug my elbows and shudder. "How would that even work?"

Willow glares, befuddled, amazed by my stupidity. "Jesus Christ, Jana. You're as bad as Macy. You only legally marry one, and the others are your unofficial husbands." She emphasizes unofficial with rabbit ears.

"Hey!" Macy objects to being lumped in with me.

"So, enough bullshit. What the hell was it like?" She wags her eyebrows and lifts her cup of coffee to her lips, slurping loudly to Macy's horror.

I cover my laugh with my hand while Macy sways in her seat. "The foursome? None of your damn business. That's privileged information."

Willow narrows her gaze. "I can't believe you'd withhold after dragging me out of bed on a Sunday morning. At least tell me if you're in love."

My heart stops, then slowly picks up speed, like a Formula One race car changing gears in the Monte Carlo Grand Prix. In love? I clench my thighs and envision coming home to all three. It's not an unpleasant thought, but how could I keep up with them every day for the rest of my life?

And how would I recover from that kind of heartbreak? Jeremy's break was hardly a blip on the screen. I couldn't wait to ditch that dead weight. If I get used to the Valerians, if I fall any harder than I already have, I may never be the same again.

Macy's right about one thing. I can't separate my emotions from sex. That's not who I am. Two nights and I feel altered, changed forever by three men who charged into my life and turned it topsy turvy. I can't allow this to continue. I'll have to set boundaries.

"Where did you go, champ?" Willow nudges my forearm. "Are you picturing your foursome? God knows, I am." She shakes her shoulders and giggles. "Are you still seeing them?"

"You're playing with fire, Jana." Macy offers a stern warning by waving her teaspoon at me.

I strike her judgmental spoon with mine. "Yes, I'm still

seeing them. We work together, and this job is important for the employees at Penrose. As soon as they're good, I'll rethink my future prospects. But no, I don't plan on engaging in sexual congress with them anymore. I'm keeping things professional and above board." I take a sip of chocolate and clink my spoon on the edge.

"So, what are you saying? No sex?" Willow attempts to clarify.

I grind my teeth, fearing I've boxed myself into a corner. "Yes!" I swipe a cookie off Macy's plate and placate myself with sugar. "No fucking sex!"

Chapter 12

Jana

"**O**pen up."

"No, it's too big for heaven's sake. You'll dislocate my jaw."

Ilya Valerian never quits, but it's too early in the morning for this kind of temptation. I lift my pumps off the floor and spin my chair to face the saltwater aquarium Vlad installed in my office on Monday. He wanted me to have one to match his own. It's gorgeous. Almost as gorgeous as the man trying to shove a whole chocolate-covered donut into my mouth---but not quite.

"I saw you inhale one of these in the employee lounge." He lies then tears the donut in half. It was a chocolate mini-muffin, and he knows it. "Are you going to deny it?"

I yank the severed piece and grab a napkin from the bag he placed on my desk. "Why are you bringing me sweets so early in the morning? Maxim brings me fruit or bagels. Vlad brings mimosas."

He tries to smile, but one bushy eyebrow jumps with annoyance. "Vlad is trying to ply you with alcohol, and Maxim is simply grasping at straws. He has no idea what women eat for breakfast." He straightens his legs and rises from his squatting position.

"And you think women eat chocolate donuts?" I chuckle and roll my chair, tucking it back into my desk.

He leans forward and grips my headrest, placing his lips to my ear. "I think you should do whatever makes you feel good, Jana. Did I make you feel good, baby?"

My nipples tighten. This is the fifth time in four days he's shamelessly crossed the line after our heated discussion on Monday. I came into work locked and loaded, believing I'd end the sordid part of our relationship for good. They responded by pulling the rug out from under me and suggesting I move into their three-story Tribeca penthouse as soon as possible. There was no sense in wasting any more time when we knew everything we ever wanted was right in front of us.

How audacious---and so damn hot.

Their offer blew my favorite pair of slingback pumps clear off my body, but I'm not one to fly by the seat of my pants. At least not on a Monday morning. Last Friday, I followed my heart and other nether regions, but I need to listen to my brain, too. I've asked for time to think it over. Lust doesn't automatically translate to love, and I'm not so sure I can tear my heart in three directions. That's a big ask for any woman.

"None of your business. These are business hours, and we agreed to only discuss business during business hours." I brush him away like a bothersome gnat and return to my work. "Your brother and I have a meeting across town at 11:00, and I'd like to finish answering my emails before we leave."

"Brother? Which one?" Ilya props his behind onto my desk, planting it centimeters from my screen. It's one of his best assets. All the Valerian men are exceptionally gifted in that region. I don't know how I get any work done. These heartless men tease me daily, taunting me with their perfect bodies and swoon-worthy stunts. I can't believe I've fallen under their spell so fast. I hang enraptured on every word and leave work every afternoon with nothing but a fat paycheck and moist panties. I ignore the beat of my racing heart and read my email out loud, hoping he won't catch me peeking at his attributes.

"Maxim," I whisper, squinting so hard my vision blurs and blots out the obscene bulge padding the front of his trousers. Good Lord, he's truly incorrigible, and I'm awful to encourage him. There's just something delicious about brazen bad boys, and Ilya's the worst. He's the brother I know the best and the easiest to be around. He's a hot beef-cake nerd who's too good to be true until you realize he's probably impossible to tie down. Except he wants to be tied down to me. But for how long?

Every morning he comes into my office to check on my progress, but I'm not so sure I've given it any serious thought. How can I move in with three men? It's been five days, and my lady parts haven't fully recovered from our thirty-six-hour romp. I'm tense, sore, and horny at the drop of a hat. And as much as I love Ilya's company, his constant presence only makes things worse. He's a horrible reminder of what might come. If I let down my defenses and follow my heart, I could spend the rest of my life in some perpetual orgy. No, that's not supposed to turn me on.

"I never promised anything, kitten. You're avoiding the inevitable and making everyone's life difficult. We belong together. I know you know it." I try to ignore his comment, but the hunger in his voice makes me clench my thighs.

"It's not that simple." I stutter and stare wide-eyed,

fearful I'll give in quicker than he has time to tear off my skirt. It's so wrong to encourage him, but I can't help my current affliction. I've got a bad case of the Valerian flu.

"Yes, it is. You're ours, baby. I've already admitted I'm in love with you. You don't need to confess you feel the same--- not yet. But you should at the very least admit you're dying to take us together again." He wags his eyebrows and smirks.

I gasp and shove his ample behind off my desk. "That's enough from you. I'm telling Vlad about your sexual harassment, mister." I pretend to balk then slump into my computer, giggling into my hair like a teenage girl.

He leans forward, grasps both sides of my head, and kisses my forehead, chuckling as he heads for the door. "I'll see you tonight, sweetheart."

"Tonight? I haven't agreed to see you tonight."

Figures.

Chapter 13

Jana

I t isn't easy being a woman in business. No matter what anyone says, it's still a boys' club, and the higher you go up the ladder, the less your peers take you seriously. Most of the time, I hardly notice. Two minutes into our meeting, Maxim takes exception.

I can tell by his stunned expression he's never experienced anything like it. The Valerian brothers are close, closer than any siblings I've ever met. They built their company together and probably schmoozed their way from meeting to meeting with only themselves in tow. Maxim leads the finance department, and most of the executives that work under him are men---an issue I addressed with Vlad two days ago. Although to be fair, Ilya's department is packed to the gills with women.

I'm not sure what I expect when I arrive side by side with Maxim Valerian, the wealthiest and most powerful man in the room. But media investors and financiers are old guard, conservative men. Their round eyes and slack jaws say everything I need to know. Despite my experience and long-standing connection to mass media, my presence is clearly unwanted.

The snubbing is subtle at first. No handshakes or eye contact. Everyone dotes on Maxim, but no one offers me a drink. Fortunately, Maxim is far more chivalrous than our hosts. Before the meeting begins, he stands to grab me a bottle of water, delicately scolding the group for failing to cater to his colleague.

Murmurs commence, but no one apologizes. It's par for the course.

The first time someone speaks over me, Maxim grits his teeth, clenching his fist on the table for everyone to see. "Miss Penrose has the floor. Please allow her to complete her sentence before you rudely jump in."

I place my hand over his forearm and smile, unwilling to ruin negotiations over something so dumb. I'm accustomed to it. I shouldn't be, but I am.

His shoulder meets mine as he cocks his head and whispers, "We can leave. You don't need to put up with this disrespect. I wouldn't tolerate it, and neither should you."

I shake my head and urge him to calm down. As much as I appreciate his chivalry, it solves nothing. We'll only lose investors for Valiant Media. None of these men will turn over a new leaf because Maxim Valerian put them in their place.

"Calm down, cowboy. This is nothing new. It's happened before, and it'll happen again. Let's just get through this bullshit for the sake of Valiant and celebrate when we're done. Launching this company means a lot to me, and I don't want to let them ruin it." I clear my throat and urge him to answer someone's question. I know the answer and could probably provide a more thorough reply, but I refer to his pseudo-expertise for the sake of my sanity.

Maxim won't have it. He shakes his head and turns to me, insisting I explain the finer points of the escalating downtrend in cable media and uptick in digital real estate over the last six years. I hesitate, but he nudges me under the table until I open my mouth and detail the latest demographics and market trends. I don't get far. Seconds into my presentation, a side conversation begins. And then another. The host, who sat as quiet as a church mouse while Maxim rambled nonsense, waves his hand to speed me up, dismissing everything I have to say before I finish.

I straighten my papers and slide them into my folder, too furious to continue and too frazzled to anticipate Maxim's next move.

"We're done here." Maxim's booming voice silences the man who cut me off. "Consider these negotiations closed and any pending business you have with Valerian Enterprises null and void." He stands from the table, helps me out of my chair, and rushes me out of the room. We can't leave soon enough.

"Maxim! You don't have to do this!" Standing by the elevators, I fuss with my bags, slide my purse over one shoulder then tuck my portfolio under my arm. "They're jerks, but they'll do anything if it's got your name attached to it. Your name makes money, and that's all they care about."

He appears unmoved by my words, mumbling under his breath while he taps the button furiously and tries to will the car to open. Down the hall, doors fly open, and a ruckus of footsteps charges towards us. Men who never apologize for anything beg Maxim's forgiveness but offer no words of contrition for me. And it doesn't go unnoticed.

"You can't lose your temper every time that happens, or we'll never get anything done. Those investors don't know jack shit about media. They just want their name tangled up with yours." I spot our car by the curb and march ahead, grateful for his chivalry but angry he's set us behind. Penrose Media is dead in the water. But Valiant, the new company Vlad's creating from its ashes, will take on many of my father's former employees. And I need to make this work for them."

Max's long strides quickly catch me. "Jana, we'll make Valiant work with or without them. But no one fucking disrespects you like that. Not in front of me. Not fucking ever." He groans with frustration and nearly slams into my back when we reach the car together. "I couldn't stay. A few more minutes, and I might have strangled him." He waves his driver away, opening the door and helping me into the backseat.

We sit in silence on opposite ends of the seat as we pull away from the curb. I understand his annoyance with the men. I wanted to jump on the table, kick them in the teeth and yell, *I am woman, hear me roar*. But what good would that do? My father's old workers need jobs more than I need to have my ego stroked. I know I'm an intelligent and capable woman. It's nice that Max knows it too, and that's enough for me. For now, anyway.

"Thank you for having my back. I appreciate it. Lots of men don't even notice when their female co-workers are being dismissed, and you did. That means a lot to me." I walk my hand across the leather seat and clasp it over his, giving it a gentle squeeze. "I'm sorry I snapped."

"Please, don't apologize." His dark gaze falls on mine, and the look in his eyes is unmistakable. He licks his lips, and I tense, fearful I've set something in motion.

"Jana..." his voice emerges like a feral groan, an inaudible whisper that makes my skin prickle. I shimmy back, bracing myself against the car door as he approaches like a jungle cat, a deadly jaguar with perfect hair and peppermint breath.

"Max," I rasp, holding my arm out to keep him at bay. "I just need a bit more time."

He brings my fingers to his lips, kissing each one, suckling my fingertips until I whimper and make a pathetic attempt to pull it away. "You're thinking about this all wrong." Maxim's dark eyes dance, and his lips curve into a knowing smile. He clasps my hand and holds it to his chest. "You can't help the way your brain is wired. You won't give yourself permission to love us together. But that's exactly what we want. It won't be perfect, and not every day will be the same. Some days will be like Club Sin, and others, we may fall asleep in front of the television. But we'll love you better together. We know you're the one, Jana. Let yourself love us together."

Chapter 14

Maxim

"**M**ax, don't tell the others. Not yet." Jana peeks over her shoulder, hoping to buy my silence by holding her naked pussy over my head.

"Of course." I position her on her knees, then finish slipping off her panties. A yellow glow of sunlight shining through the back windshield illuminates her arousal and makes my mouth water for a taste.

I spread her legs wider and tuck my head between her thighs. Her musky scent makes my cock dig into my zipper and begs me to come out to play. I drag my tongue down her slit and lap up the sweet honey I've been craving all week. "Do you want me to stop?" I ask with no real intention of forfeiting my place at her pussy.

She shudders and falls forward, catching herself on the armrest. "No, but can you keep our secret?" She cries out when I lash her clit once, twice, three times before I answer the only way I know how. "That's unlikely." I bury my face in her wet warmth, suckling her clit, massaging it between my lips until her thighs tremble and her hums turn to cries of palpable yearning for my cock.

"Max! Holy shit, not so fast!" She yelps and wiggles her ass, feeding her pussy straight into my mouth. That probably wasn't her plan, but once she starts, she can't stop. And neither can I. The more she gives, the more I take, the more I want. When I find her perfect spot, the one I know will trap her in my web, I strike without mercy and catch her by surprise.

Her trembling knees give way. She bangs her fists into the leather seats as her body spins into a shattering dance of tiny jerks and calls to Jesus. Jana clutches her throat, frightened by her she-wolf howls and mumbles for mercy through her quivering lips. I top her off with a growl, inhaling every drop of her thick honey, and unbuckle my belt. My throbbing cock needs to feel her pussy spasm around me. I need to sink as far as she'll take me and unload until I have nothing left to give.

"Hold on, please." She gasps, stammering through labored breaths as she tries to gather her thoughts. "What if I can't, Max? What if you're all too much for me?"

"Too much?" I continue to unzip, tugging my dress shirt out of my slacks and unfastening the rest of the buttons.

She nods, clasping her hands with worry. "I don't know if I can keep up. Not forever. You'll get tired and want someone else." She waits for me to comment, but I'm too busy tearing the shirt off my back.

"Well?" She rises to her knees and tries to read my expression. If she interprets anything but mad lust, she's read me wrong.

I shake my head and grab the hem of her dress, pulling it over her head in one good yank. "Don't' be ridiculous. You're twelve years younger than Ilya and me and sixteen years younger than Vlad. With your energy, you'll bury us all and find three more men to entertain you in your golden years." I trail my hands up the sharp angle of her waist and greedily cup both breasts. The weight of her soft flesh in my hands makes the corners of my lips tug upward. My heart flutters with love---boundless, unfettered love that wants to be unleashed to its full potential.

"I love you, Jana. We love you. And I know you're falling in love with us. Let yourself fall, or we'll push you over that cliff." I seal my lips to hers and trap her in my grateful arms. "Now, stop talking and turn over that pussy. It's been five days, and I'm tired of using my hand."

Aroused by my words, her lips find mine, and her tongue invades my mouth. She captures my bottom lip and suckles it between her teeth, teasing me with tiny kisses that drive me mad. She pulls away and smiles, but I crush my mouth to hers and deepen our kiss. The old Jana was tethered too long. This Jana has the fire of a thousand suns burning inside her. Now that she knows what she's missed, it'll take all three of us to make her happy.

"Max... it's been so long." Her sweet words propel me into action. I lift her into my arms and straddle her over my lap. Her naked pussy lands next to my stiff cock, and my breath hitches, tortured by the touch of her wet heat. Overcome by lust and the sight of her naked body, I encase my face in her breasts and ravish what belongs to me.

"Is this what you want?" I slip inside her tight walls and watch her eyes startle wide with each inch of my invasion.

"It's been too long," she whispers and wraps her arms around my neck, lifting her knees and impaling herself deep. When she roots herself at my balls, my eyes roll back in my head, and my heart leaps into my throat. I thread my fingers through her long dark hair and bring my fevered gaze forward. Her eyes find mine, and I choke out the words, "you're ours, Jana. I won't let you get away."

"Max!" she gasps and arches back, thrusting her hips forward as my cock touches just the right spot inside her. She screams, vibrating in the throes of ecstasy, and digs her nails into my skin. I flip her over and push her knees to her shoulders, thrusting into her tight channel until I hit the spot that makes her wail.

"Maxim!" Her toes curl, and her voice suddenly climbs to an immeasurable octave. I know she needs more, and I haven't even scratched the surface of this unquenchable hunger.

While she trembles beneath me, basking in a state of blissful afterglow, we arrive at her place, and I carry her in. Here, we start from the beginning. We take it sweet and slow, and I promise to keep her secret for a few more days.

I should have known that wasn't possible.

Chapter 15

Jana

This is so unprofessional. Maxim called us out of the office as soon as we arrived at my apartment. He's allowed to do things like that. No one questions a Valerian. But this is my first full week, and office gossip spreads like wildfire. It's bad enough I have a sweet office in the executive wing, catty-corner from Vlad's. That did not go unnoticed with the hordes of female employees who have probably pursued that man for years, but I've heard whispers people believe we're having an affair.

It's reckless hearsay, and I don't want this afternoon romp to add fuel to the fire. I mean, of course, it's true, but they have no proof.

"Where are you going?" Maxim stirs awake with a shift in the mattress. I woke up thirty minutes ago, but he was sleeping so peacefully with one arm wound tightly around my waist, I felt terrible waking him up. Unfortunately, nature calls.

"I'll be right back. Go back to sleep." I slither out of bed, shrug on Maxim's undershirt, and pad into the bathroom. It was nice being alone with Max. Three at once feels sexy as hell, but one at a time helps me see them as individuals. As much as they talk about loving them together, I still need to fall in love with three separate men, and I can't do that if I don't get to know them separately. I think I'd like to see Ilya and Vlad alone before I make up my mind. That's the least they can give me.

"Dear Lord, I look like death warmed over." I stare into the mirror and see smeared red lipstick spread across my cheek. Things may have gotten out of hand. I can't believe Max didn't tell me. After pulling up my hair and washing the makeup off my face, I step into the bedroom to check on him.

"Are you hungry?" When the sound of snoring greets me, I take that as a no. But I'm starving. It's nearly 5:00, and we skipped lunch in exchange for strenuous physical activity. I don't think I can wait for him to wake up.

Starving and sure I'm woozy from low blood sugar, I slip out of the room and head towards the kitchen. I don't like asking Max to withhold information from his brothers. They're close for a reason, and I don't want to come between them. Today wasn't a mistake. I needed this more than I realized. I'll talk to Vlad and Ilya today. I'll confess what happened as a statement of record. It's not like we did anything wrong. We just jumped the gun and got a bit ahead of ourselves. If anything, they should thank Max for making me turn a corner.

That sounds like an excellent way to start. They understand rational thinking and the need to process your thoughts. Well, Vladimir does.

"Don't move a fucking muscle." A hand clasps tightly over my mouth and drags me into the living room. My heart races. Adrenaline rushes through my veins as fight or flight kicks into high gear.

"You've been a bad girl, kitten." I thrash and growl with rage until the sound of his voice and the scent of his cologne sink into my brain and force me to look over my shoulder.

"You idiot." I groan and squirm to free myself from his grasp. But he doesn't give an inch. "Max is sleeping, Ilya. This isn't funny. How the hell did you get in here anyway?"

He kneels me on the sofa and places my hands on the armrest. "You like role play, kitten. I let myself in." With one thrust, he sinks his thick member deep into my core. I fall forward and clutch the end table, clinging to the smooth mahogany as he plunges in and out, harder, deeper, wilder with an animalistic grunt that makes my hair stand on end.

"Tell me you love me, Jana." He leans forward, reaches over my hip, and gently strokes my clit. "Tell me you love me. I can't live without you."

"Ilya!" I'm so close. Each thrust gets me inches away. Every stroke of his finger brings me to the brink of explosion. But he withholds my climax. Like a naughty priest, he wants to hear my confession before he grants me the ultimate absolution.

"If you can't say it, you don't deserve to come, baby." He sets a brutal pace, plunging with anger and ramming his enormous cock into my quivering pussy to teach me just how badly I've behaved. I cry for mercy, then grind back, welcoming every thrust like a wanton woman who's lost her way and has no need for directions.

"Please, Ilya. I'm not ready." I can say it. I could say it a thousand times, but I'm a greedy woman who wants angry sex.

"Then I'll make you ready." He flips me over onto my back and pushes my knees to my shoulders. I'm so wet, I'm soaked to my thighs, and he can see it all. A voyeur at heart, he watches his cock slip inside me, grinning with wicked delight at the sight of our union. It's almost too much to bear. His pace returns to a reckless speed. His fingers find my clit and stroke to the beat of his rutting cock, thrusting seamlessly through my wet slit and taking me to a world where I leave my body and fly high above the stars.

"Come with me, Jana. Tell me you love me. I know you do." He asks again, and I have to give in. He knows I love having sex with him, but he should know I love him. Men need to hear it too.

I'm not ready to decide, but he should know I love him.

"I love you." My true release comes with my confession. "I love you, Ilya."

He fists his hand into my hair and snakes his arms around my back. His full lips smother mine, ravaging me in a kiss that reverberates through my heart and settles into my soul.

"That's my good girl. Let's wake up Maxim."

Chapter 16

Vlad

"**Y**ou dirty, dirty girl." I pull Jana into her foyer and slam the door behind us. We said one goodnight kiss, and I swear I meant it. She made the request before dinner, and as much as it killed me to keep intimacy off the menu, I kept to her rules. Jana isn't a conquest to win. She'll be our partner in life, and a partner should be respected. If she needs more time, I need to give her space to consider the gravity of her decision.

We've waited years for her to come along, never believing she truly existed. Waiting a few more days or, God forbid, weeks to resume our relationship isn't an enormous sacrifice. I know my brothers agree. Well, Maxim agrees. Ilya won't give her any peace.

But that was before she tried my patience and turned into a brat.

"Daddy, you promised!" She tears her lips off my neck and pulls her hand out from my jeans. That was my breaking point. The second she unzipped my jeans and stuck her hand inside my boxers, Jana Penrose nullified all earlier agreements of abstinence and guaranteed the games were on.

"You know what you're doing, little girl." I tug off my belt and crack the leather strap against the wall. She kicks off her heels and tosses one in my direction, giggling as she makes her way down her darkened hallway. "I'm coming to get you, even if I have to tear down that fucking door. Nothing's keeping me from destroying that pussy, Jana." For fuck's sake, I can't believe the shit that's coming out of my mouth. But there's just something about this girl that brings out my inner beast.

"Forget it, Daddy. All I wanted to do was feel it. It was your job to stop me." Her playful voice makes me want to race into her arms, but I take my time and draw out the suspense. She teased me all through dinner, hoping I'd break my promise. And I don't think I'm flattering myself. Her game of footsies was sweet, and although it got me hard, I took it as nothing more than a frisky way to move the conversation along. I'm not an oaf incapable of controlling my urges.

I felt backing her ass into my hips and rubbing her cheeks against my erection while we waited for the valet was unnecessary. But I figured she was being a brat and testing my patience. Her hand on my thigh while I drove her home got my juices flowing, but still, I kept my cool, and I swore I'd see this through. I never expected her to take such drastic steps.

But if my lady wants dick, my lady shall have it.

"Vlad?" I stay silent and drag my feet across the Persian rug, littered with remnants of her wardrobe. While I stalk my prey like a creepy villain in a horror movie, I pull off my sweater, tug off my boots and discard my jeans. "Are you there?" She calls again, fearing I've left her naked and horny. Not a chance, sweetheart.

I reach her door and find it cracked open, only a dim light shining within. "Daddy's here, baby. He's not going anywhere. And neither are you." I walk through, and my lonely heart skips a beat when her soft voice guides me towards the center of the room.

"I'm right here." She steps into the candlelight, naked as the day she was born, and my heart quickens to such a reckless pace, my vision blurs. I can't believe how quickly I've fallen in love. If it was happening to anyone else, I'd never believe it. We've already had sex in every way imaginable, but this is our first real date alone. Maybe we should have done this from the start, but I didn't expect things to fall into place so soon.

I reach out in the dark, following the scent of her skin, and taste her on my breath. "I love you, Jana. You know, don't you?" I close the distance between us and pull her into my chest. Her breasts spill into my large hands, filling them to capacity, and I plunder each one with my greedy mouth.

"Daddy..." she purrs like a kitten, and her skin turns to gooseflesh in my hands. I lick each taut nipple, suckling without mercy as she dances on the balls of her feet, losing strength from the wild sensations ravaging her limbs. Fearing her knees will buckle, I wrap her legs around my waist and carry us onto the bed.

I clasp my hands to hers and hold them over her head. My lips fall on hers, and our mouths mate with a longing I never imagined feeling. My heart recognized Jana the moment we met. The spark was instant and unmistakable, and the minute we made love, everything fell into place, like I knew it would.

"How can you think of leaving us? Don't you know how

miserable we'll be without you?" We gaze into each other's eyes, lost in a moment of wonder and mutual lust. She flutters her lashes, an innocent gesture meant to throw me off.' "What if everything falls apart? How will I ever stop loving you?"

"Do you love me?" My heart thumps like a bass drum and sends throbbing vibrations into my ears. I sweep her into my arms and seal our lips in a blistering kiss that summons visions of babies, birthday parties, and walks on the beach. I want to know every part of this girl, and she needs to meet every inch of me---over and over until the end of time.

She thrills me with a soft yes, and our eyes lock in a moment that seals both our fates. Jana loves me. She loves me, and if she doesn't already love Ilya and Max, I know she will. None of us have ever done this before. We're embarking on something new, something we need that only the other can give us.

But right now, I need Jana. I need to listen to her voice hit that high note of ecstasy, and I want to know I'm responsible for taking her there. Tonight, for the first time, I have her all to myself.

I kiss my way down the soft curve of her breasts across her abdomen and work my way to the apex of her thighs. The smell of her sex reaches my nostrils, and my taste buds melt. She's the best pussy I've ever had, and these last six days have been nothing less than torture.

I lower my mouth and suckle on her tight bundle of nerves, licking like the greediest glutton who hordes his ice cream on a warm August day. Her arousal drips into my mouth, and the taste turns me feral. I lose my composure, and my mind quickly follows. She can't send me away. She doesn't need more time. Another week without my Jana will only drive me mad.

I slide my hands under her ass and lift her pussy straight into my mouth, stunning her with my avarice. She screams obscenities and cries for a short reprieve but refrains from using our safe word. I give her nothing but tongue. I feed recklessly, thrashing her clit, laving, licking, petting with hummingbird speed until she tumbles into an obscene frenzy of electric ecstasy that flattens her to the mattress. The sight nearly takes my breath away.

"Vlad..." she weeps openly and holds the sheets for purchase. "That wasn't fair."

I drag my body over hers and swirl my tongue around her taut nipple, relishing the feel of her supple skin against my beard. "Now you know how it feels, sweetheart. I've been dead these last six days. I want to give you space, my love. You deserve time and space. You should have months to figure this out because we're going to overwhelm the hell out of you. But I just can't bear it. Come home to us. We need you."

She chuckles and rolls to her side, letting her long dark hair fall on my face. For a moment, I lose myself in the smell of her perfume and imagine years into the future. I'm not leaving here without her.

"I am home, Vlad."

"Your home is with us. Do you want me to call Ilya and Max to help convince you?"

She giggles into my chest and sighs, "Just Max. Ilya is probably waiting for me in the kitchen. I'll go get him."

Chapter 17

Epilogue - Two Years Later

Ilya

"**A**re you ready? Do you have your uniform washed and ready to go? The car is picking us up in fifteen minutes." I tap my watch and carry Nadia into Vladimir's outstretched arms, allowing him to give her a kiss goodnight before we leave. We're due to meet Jana at Club Sin in thirty minutes, and I don't want to be late. Although they know her well, I hate the idea of anyone believing she's a free agent. The thought alone makes me want to choke the life out of every horny bastard there.

"Be a good girl for Papa." Vlad kisses his infant daughter on the head, nuzzles her cheek then hands her to her nanny. As the pair heads towards the nursery, Maxim chases them into the hall and gives our niece a goodbye hug. Nadia is only technically Vlad's daughter. We love her and raise her like she's our own, but paternity was a sticking point for Jana. If we wanted to start a family, she insisted her children know who they called Daddy and who they called Uncle Max or Uncle Vlad.

We share a wife, but her babies wouldn't share a father. Fair enough. Whatever Jana wants, Jana gets. That's a motto that makes our lives fuller, richer, and so much sweeter.

"Are you sure this is for Jana and not some strange fantasy you have about cheerleaders?" Maxim lifts the garment bag holding the specially designed football uniforms I ordered last month for Jana's private twenty-fifth birthday party.

I shove him towards the door and wave my hand to rush Vlad off his phone. "Do you have any idea how hard it is to find football uniforms in our sizes? I'm 6'7 ---those are NFL sizes. This is a one-time use, and it's all part of the fantasy. Last Christmas, Macy told me Jana always wanted to be a cheerleader. She said she and Willow were cheerleaders, but Jana wasn't allowed to try out---some bullshit about her father. Poor Jana attended all their games, memorized their cheers, and regretted not joining the squad. Well, tonight, my baby is going to be a cheerleader." I lift my second garment bag, unzip it and reveal Jana's uniform.

"So why the fuck are we football players? Why aren't we male cheerleaders? We could have helped her do a few cheers." Vlad injects his two cents as we head into the elevator. "And why did she have to meet us there? You know I hate when she goes without us."

I shake my head with disgust. "Get a grip. What woman wants to bang three male cheerleaders? We're football players. Her uniform says head cheerleader because my baby is the fucking best, and if she'd tried out, she would have been head cheerleader, not that know-it-all Macy." I walk ahead of my brothers and make a beeline for the car. I've got nothing against Macy. She's a sweetheart. I'm just a competitive jerk, and that spills over to anything pertaining to Jana.

We each married Jana in our own way two months after we got together, but the only legal one is her marriage to

Vladimir. It was the practical choice for the sake of our family and future children. Vlad is the oldest, and more than half of our assets are under his name. As Vlad's wife, Jana's future will always be secure.

But we don't like to think of that. Jana belongs to the three of us. We share her separately, and we share her together. And, of course, we belong to her. Tonight is all about her. I really hope she gets a kick out of it.

"Mr. Valerian, what took you so long?" The beautiful woman in red rushes to greet us with open arms and a killer dress that shows off far too much leg. She sneaks her hands into my coat and wraps her arms around my waist. Her dark eyes flash to mine, and I lose my heart all over again.

"Mrs. Valerian, where the hell did you get that dress?" I give her a disapproving glare and smack her ass.

"Maxim bought it for me. It's a birthday present!" She moves on to Max and seals her lips to his, giving him a much warmer greeting than she gave me.

"She looks beautiful. What are you complaining about?" Maxim flashes the key to Room Four, our regular room, and the one with a particular piece of furniture installed explicitly for tonight's visit.

"My love, don't you look debonair." Jana twirls into Vlad's arms and gives him a tender kiss on his lips. Sometimes I think she does it on purpose.

"Sweetheart." I lift the key and extend my hand for her to take. Jana rushes to my side, adjusts her dress, and changes her tune. As we walk down the red corridor, her eyes dance with curiosity. She knew we were coming here and planned something special, but I kept everyone in the dark until today.

Before we enter the room, I hand her a garment bag with her name. "This is for you. Don't ruin your surprise by looking around. Go into the changing room, and we'll wait for you in the bedroom."

Her eyes grow wide. Her feet pitter-patter on the floor like a kid on Christmas morning. When the door swings open, she disappears into the fitting room while we strip as fast as we can and try to shove our old asses into tight pants, jerseys, and cleats.

As I expect and secretly wished, we hear a squeal of delight. "Oh, my God. You didn't! Head cheerleader!" Jana fumbles in the tiny room, stripping, dressing, and reappearing only seconds after we've tied our shoes. We gasp together. Stunned by her beauty and amazed at how big our erections look in tight white pants.

Her black and red pleated skirt is only long enough to cover her ass. The tight-fitted short sleeve sweater with the letter V on it was my idea. And fixing her hair into a high ponytail pulls the whole outfit together. She's the hottest cheerleader I've ever seen.

"Who did this?!" She twirls and taps her cheer sneakers in a fit of excitement, then wipes an errant tear off her left cheek. My heart flutters with love. She's the most beautiful girl in the world.

"Ilya planned the whole thing. He deserves all the credit." Vlad answers her question and prevents me from singing my own praises.

Jana's face beams bright with joy, the kind of joy I only ever see when she holds Nadia. "Thank you!" She flies into my arms and climbs my legs like a tree. I wrap her legs around my hips and sit her ass in my hands. "You're welcome. I hope you have one less regret, kitten."

She nods and hugs my neck. "You don't know what this means to me."

"It's not over. We expect cheers, Jana." I place her on the

floor and hand her a pair of pompoms. And when you're done--" I walk to the far end of the room and pull the tarp off the specially supplied piece of furniture. "When you're done, the three of us are taking our naughty cheerleader back here."

She covers her mouth, fifty percent horrified but one hundred percent titillated, if I know my girl. "Did you have someone build a replica of the back of the school bus?"

I wag my eyebrows and nod. "I did, indeed. So, let's get some cheers for your football players. Because I've heard rumors that the head cheerleader takes it in the ass."

* * *

JANA

"We'll get caught. I know we'll get caught," I rasp, breathless from kisses as three men surround and undress me in the back of the bus. Max pulls off my skirt and panties. Vlad strips me naked from the waist up. Someone spreads my legs from behind and slides a lubed cock between my cheeks. I look over my shoulder. It's Ilya.

I shake my head and pretend I'm a shy teenage girl instead of a married woman with three husbands who does this at least once a week. "I can't! I don't know how."

Ilya takes it slow and goes along with the act. He helps me along, holding steady while I get used to the feeling of his invasion. I shiver, pretending the stimulation is too much to bear, moaning quietly as he slides in an inch at a time and begging off when it becomes too much cock for a cheerleader to take.

We build a quiet rhythm that slowly builds into a tight tension. Ilya drives harder, pistoning in and out with a steady brutality that he knows I enjoy. I grind back, wiggling my ass into him, meeting him halfway with a passionate enthusiasm I know he loves. Our hunger escalates into animalistic rutting that leaves no room for anyone but us. He leans forward and cups my breasts, using my body to steady his onslaught. Ilya's incomparable. I welcome everything he has to give and revel in my destruction. With three more strokes, I feel the first eruption. Two more, and we explode like two volcanoes, leaving nothing but ash in our wake. This is turning out to be one of the best birthdays ever.

"You're not quitting yet." Vlad and Max stand over us, stiff and ready to go.

"I'm a mom now. Give me five minutes."

THANK YOU FOR READING!

Room Nine

For Their Eyes Only

club sin
new
orleans

ROOM NINE

For Their Eyes Only

MATILDA MARTEL

Chapter One

Andrei

Sooner or later, your past catches up with you.

Today is that day.

I slip my cell phone from my coat pocket and grimace at the message on the screen. It's an address on the other side of the bridge, a neighborhood in Brooklyn I haven't frequented since my mother moved to Florida a few years ago.

Nothing left there but a handful of old friends, a few enemies, and horrible memories I'd love to forget.

"Looks like we're headed to Little Odessa." I hand the address to my driver, Olav, who seamlessly changes courses west. I'm unsure why we have to meet in such a conspicuous place. Boris Volkov resides on the periphery of every law enforcement officer in New York.

I left that world behind five years ago and fought hard to rebuild my life on the right side of the law. The last thing I want is to get caught up in a sting and wind up on the FBI's hit list.

Part of my job is maintaining a friendly and stable relationship with law enforcement. If anyone catches me fraternizing with Volkov, it could jeopardize everything.

I listen to the tires thump over the imbalanced asphalt, the familiar sound of crossing the Brooklyn Bridge, and steer my gaze to the choppy waters of the East River. The rocking motion brings a tinge of nostalgia, as if I'm traveling back in time, growing younger by the second.

If only that were possible. There are so many things I'd do differently the second time around.

We cross into the borough and take a shortcut through Brooklyn Heights on our way to Bell Parkway. The highway saves us time, but we're still forty-five minutes away from our destination, an upscale bar called Sergei's, owned by Boris' younger brother. Unlike everyone else in Volkov's extended family, Sergei didn't follow in their father's footsteps, preferring to live a comfortable, crime-free life with his family in the old neighborhood. But he'll never be truly free. You never stop looking over your shoulder when you're tied to the bratva.

I told Boris I wanted to meet on neutral ground. This must be his pathetic attempt at appeasing my request while keeping his advantage. He hasn't changed a bit.

Few people know of my former affiliation with the Volkov family. I operated from the shadows, maintained anonymity, and never paid for my crimes. I shed those shackles when I walked away from that world, taking my younger brothers with me. Together we reemerged as entrepreneurs specializing in security and surveillance, cashing in on the many skills we learned as bratva assassins and fixers.

Vadim, Viktor, and I pooled our resources and went into business for ourselves. It took two years to make a profit, but eventually, our work paid off. Fortunately, we secured government contracts and international clients who pay top dollar. We're not a household name, but the kind of people who need our services know how to find us.

"What do you suppose he wants?" Olav drops his speed as we approach Brighton Beach Avenue, minutes from our destination.

"I have no idea. Boris wouldn't share details over the phone. He's just as paranoid as always." I roll my eyes and check my messages, hoping he's had a change of heart, and decided to call someone else. We haven't done business in so long. I don't know why he'd trust me with anything important. Men like Volkov believe they can procure anything they need with the right amount of money. They typically do. But I don't need his money. I've got plenty of my own.

"I don't think you'll have to wait too long to find out," Olav offers a few words of comfort before exiting the vehicle to open my door. He's always been more of a body-guard than a driver, and since I was only allowed to bring one man with me, I chose the biggest, burliest bastard I know.

"You're right. Boris doesn't fuck around with words. Let's hope he makes this quick." I straighten my jacket, adjust my cuff links and lead Olav past Volkov's men into Sergei's.

Twenty minutes later, I'm sipping vodka and staring into the somber gaze of my childhood friend. My brows pulled low and ripe with judgment. "What do you mean Vivienne's gone missing? Your daughter?" My hackles rise. She can't be more than twenty, and he doesn't look nearly as panicked as he should be. The streets are overrun with his enemies. Anyone could have gotten to her.

There's something he's not telling me. Boris has a

special place in his heart for his only daughter. Unlike his son, Vasily, she's a sweet girl, too innocent for her fucked-up family and too trusting to survive among wolves. If this is true, she needs all the help she can get.

We never met. In my previous profession, I kept to the shadows and never mingled with members of the boss's family. I only met Vasily when he was old enough to join his father's ranks. But I watched her from a distance and worried she'd never reach adulthood. Volkov had the same concerns. He kept his prized jewel sheltered and guarded by a team of bodyguards, only allowing her to leave the house to attend school. Maybe she finally got tired of living in a cage.

Boris nods, then leans forward, elbows propped on the table as he sucks in a shaky breath. "We had a fight. She accused me of planning to marry her off. I promised her that wasn't true, but she didn't believe me."

A quick stream of unpleasant memories floods my brain, remembering Boris' arrangement, his horrible marriage, and the messy divorce that followed. I let out a soft chuckle and ask, "Where did she get that idea? I'm sure someone as lovely as Vivienne had a ton of offers, but I hope you wouldn't do that to her."

He immediately defends himself. "Of course not. I wouldn't put either of my children through that. It never works out. I think her mother got to her. She's always tried to drive a wedge between us."

My confusion sets in. Vivienne's mother, a woman named Charlotte Pinkerton, dated Boris briefly after his divorce. She was utterly horrible and disappeared shortly after their heated affair—after she set his car on fire. He swore he wouldn't chase her down and stayed away until he discovered she'd given birth to his daughter. He refused to let her cut him out of her life, and she happily relinquished custody of her daughter for a lump sum. I was under the impression she was still living a life of leisure in the south of France. "When the hell did Charlotte come back into her life?"

Boris grimaces, his mouth set in a thin line as he inhales half his glass of vodka. "When she was eighteen, she asked me if she could visit her mother. Of course, I was against it, but I couldn't keep my daughter from her mother. Unfortunately, Charlotte managed to worm her way back into Vivienne's life, pretending to be a doting mother. I don't know what happened or how she came to this conclusion, but days after her twenty-second birthday party, she disappeared and left nothing but a note demanding I leave her alone." He hangs his head and shakes it with remorse. "It's not a coincidence that Charlotte was in town when she disappeared. But I know she's not with her. I've had her followed nonstop since Vivi left."

"Twenty-two? When did she grow up? She was a gangly teenager the last time I saw her." I make a motion with my hand, implying she's only knee-high.

"Time flies. My little girl is a woman but still vulnerable, Andrei. I need to find her." He scrubs his salt-and-pepper beard, rubbing his jaw to alleviate the tension from clenching his teeth.

I shift in my seat and cross my arms over my chest, still confused why he's asked to see me. "Why am I here, Boris?"

He looks over his shoulder and clears his throat before dropping the volume of his voice. "I came to you because this is your area of expertise. And I trust you. Plus, Vivienne will be on the lookout for my men. She'll be looking over her shoulder for the usual suspects, but she doesn't know you. You can operate incognito and make sure she's safe."

This is an unusual request to hit me out of the blue. He's right—surveillance is my specialty, but I'm not a private investigator. Boris has billions of dollars at his disposal and can pay for a team of investigators who will cater to his every wish for the right price. I'm not one of them.

"We haven't seen one other in years, and I have minimal experience tracking people down. Why me?" I question his motives, still unable to decipher why he needs to drag me into his world over something he can handle on his own. "Surveillance doesn't mean I'm a detective."

"Because you're capable and trustworthy. I need this handled with discretion. There's a rat in my organization. I don't have any proof, but I have a short list of suspects. Vasily is working on trimming it down. I can't show a hint of weakness until I learn who's betraying me to Aleksei Grinkov. You're on the outside, and you're one of the best. I'm begging you, Andrei." Boris' stern expression softens with vulnerability. We used to be close, and I know how much he loves his children.

I take a deep breath and contemplate a decision that most likely is out of my hands. Boris is asking, but that doesn't mean he'll take no for an answer. He's a relentless bastard. It took a lot for him to lower himself to begging.

"Vasily? You just sent a bull into a china shop." I make a joke to lighten the heavy mood. "You know better than that."

Boris chuckles and tops off my vodka, clinking the glass before filling his own. "You haven't seen him in years. My boy may surprise you. Is he volatile? Of course. He's a

Volkov. But he's got a good head on his shoulders and almost always does what he's told."

"Almost always?" My brow pulls low in a questioning frown.

He offers an unconvincing smile. "Vivienne is different. She's a good girl who treats everyone with kindness. I fear her big heart will get her in trouble. She's not like Charlotte. She's far more like my mother—God rest her soul." He lifts his glass and takes a long pull from his vodka. "But she's angry with me. She wants her mother's approval, and I fear Charlotte took advantage and turned her against me. I'd never force her into an arranged marriage. You know me, Andrei. I indulge my children. Vasily is evidence of that."

I blow out a heavy breath and remove a pad and pen from my suit pocket. If we're going to keep this discreet, it's best not to use technology until I can make sure it's encrypted. "Tell me what I need to know, and I'll see what I can do." It's important not to make any promises when I'm unsure if his daughter is alive. My heart stings at the thought of Vivi coming to harm. She doesn't deserve to get caught up in her father's mess. Boris has more enemies than days of the year, and in his world, missing means dead.

Boris stands and signals his men to put some space between us and them before leading me to a table at the far end of the room. "Let's have dinner, and I'll share everything I have. Spare no expense and send me the bill when you're finished. I'd rather not leave crumbs for my rat until I know she's safe."

"No promises, Boris."

He nods and pulls my chair from the table as if he's just asked me on a date. "I know you won't disappoint me."

Chapter Two

Vivi

"Now, where did I leave off?" I recline against the arm of my loveseat and relax into an oversized pillow, wiggling into the cushion until I find a comfortable position that compliments my figure. Thousands of people watch me at any given moment, and I like to present the best version of myself.

In this business, image is everything.

Comments flood the chat box, reminding me I left off when my heroine, Ellie, was moments away from being railed by two male cult members. It seems like the morning crowd is more restless than usual. Their enthusiasm pads my wallet and I wouldn't be doing my job well if I didn't give them what they came for.

Every day, I read snippets from my many works in progress—romantic smut that I plan to one day publish. I started easy, offering slow-burn romance, building momentum, holding out on the graphic details until they were invested enough to come back for more. But angst takes time and the more popular I become the less free time I have for writing. Lately, I've rolled out the hardcore sex by the second chapter which has led to more people asking for private sessions. I need to stick with what works, so today's sample is hotter than usual.

"My horror quickly transformed into lust and curiosity. My pussy was so wet, I could hear it every time I moved, and there was no doubt in my mind they could smell how aroused I'd become. Ian spread my legs, ran his finger down my soaked slit, and watched me react to his touch. I couldn't help myself. Our lust was palpable, and his gaze kindled a fire threatening to make me go up in flames. Without a word, he dipped his head between the apex of my thighs and buried his mouth in my pussy. These men were strangers, yet I felt no desire to run away."

I read using my best impression of Marilyn Monroe, low and breathy. It's ten in the morning, but that doesn't prevent my thread from blowing up with enthusiasm.

> Albert112: Two men at once? Is that something you're into? I have a few friends who'd love to meet you.

There's always one in every bunch. While I don't advertise I'm a virgin, I make it clear that these are nothing but lust prose torn from my imagination. Some jerks simply enjoy testing boundaries. Fortunately for me, a few knights in shining armor typically come through to defend my honor.

> Gangster431: Cut the crap. Pinky's a classy lady.

> PinkysBedroom: Thanks, Gangster. You're such a gentleman.

His name should give me pause, considering what my

father does for a living, but Gangster is one of my regulars. He never asks for a private session or says anything inappropriate. Not all men want to see skin. Some enjoy watching a woman like me reading naughty stories—giving fuel to their imaginations.

I'd like to think it warms them up for the women in their lives.

I take a sip of water to clear my throat and continue reading from my spicy novella entitled, The Cult, a brief tale of a young woman's erotic journey from virginity, indoctrination, and her eventual sexual liberation. In part one, she gets involved with a cult leader that marries her off to two men. They both believe their sexual prowess will make her to surrender to a life of domesticated bliss, guaranteeing them a submissive and doting wife. She proves them wrong in part two.

An hour and a half into my live stream, I end with a wave and a kiss, then shut down my feed. I've got thirty minutes to change clothes and meet Elsa at our favorite diner on Lafayette Street. I'll never make it on time, and Lord knows that girl will be pissed. But I couldn't stop in the middle of a hot scene. It's best practice to leave subscribers on the edge of their seats and entice them to return for more. But it would have been cruel to depart in the middle of Elle's first double penetration.

My audience deserves better than that.

Twenty minutes later, I'm racing to catch a streetcar down St. Charles for my three-block trip toward Sunny's Diner. Walking would have been faster, but my mood makes me lazy. Or perhaps it's the heat. No one warned me about the crazy humidity so late in the year. It's nearly autumn, and the oppressive heat doesn't relent until late evening. I swear, most days, I feel like a wilting flower.

As the streetcar slows, I hop off and race toward Sunny's Diner and find Elsa waiting outside, scrutinizing her watch to point out the exact time of my arrival.

"Oh, my Lord, you're on time. Hell has frozen." Elsa smirks and spreads her arms for a hug. I roll my eyes and petulantly stomp into her embrace, tugging her hair to demonstrate my displeasure with her judgment.

"I'm three minutes early. You have no idea how fast I dressed to make it here on time." I point to my poorly tied Converse sneakers and the dark waves falling from my messy bun. Usually, I'd take more pride in my appearance, but I couldn't bear another of Elsa's lectures on my lack of accountability and poor organizational skills. She's such a stickler for rules.

"Yes, I can tell." Elsa pinches her nose with distaste, unimpressed with my choice of denim overalls over a tight red tank top. "Fortunately, this dive doesn't have a dress code. Let's eat." She swings the door open and allows me to pass through first, gesturing to the hostess that the rest of her party has arrived.

Sunny's Diner is a local gem I discovered days after moving to New Orleans in the spring. It's cozy, nostalgic interior reminds me of the diners I frequented with my dad when I was younger. Despite his busy life and obnoxious wealth, he tried to give us a sense of normalcy. He wanted us to know that prosperity was fleeting and the best memories were made spending time with the ones you love—not gathering possessions.

Once a week, he took the time to buy groceries on his own, rather than sending the housekeeper, and tried cooking a home-cooked meal for his children. The operative word is *tried*. My poor dad failed miserably, nearly burning down the kitchen on more than one occasion.

After he ruined dinner, he'd drive us to one of the many diners near our home in Brooklyn and we'd spend the evening talking about school and friends. Some of my best memories are of time spent in diners. They've always felt like my home away from home.

We stride across the near-empty place, my sneakers squeaking as I walk along the freshly mopped checkerboard tile floor and crawl onto the opposite side of our booth. I'm so short my legs dangle off the red leather banquette seat, causing my feet to hover two inches above the floor. I feel childish next to Elsa's tall frame and regal stature, but instead of complaining about her seat choice, I embrace my deficiencies, lift my legs, and tuck each ankle beneath my thigh.

"How's tricks?" I ask while I peruse the thick menu, my eyes ping-ponging off each page as I try to find something I've never eaten before. I abhor monotony. Every day is an opportunity to chip away at the boredom and drudgery of life. Even if it's nothing more dazzling than eating something new.

"Shouldn't I be the one asking that question?" Elsa peeks over the top of her menu, her blue eyes narrowed with misplaced judgment. Two months ago, she ditched her sweet CamLife persona, PlayingFootsies, because her controlling boyfriend considered it disrespectful. And suddenly, she's turned into the morality police.

"No, you shouldn't, *foot girl*. It's a simple question meant to ask how's the job coming along. Keep all your condemnation on that side of the table, or I'll remind you how you were the one who encouraged me to join the platform," I huff, annoyed but too hungry to argue. I'm not ashamed of what I do. It's an honest living that pays the bills with enough cushion to build a nest egg.

"I'm not saying it's bad. But you've made enough money to cut back and rejoin the real world. It was a temporary solution, not a long-term fix." Elsa changes gears, stirring her coffee as she spews bitter words. *Real world?* I adore her, but she's a walking advertisement for how much misery loves company. She hates her new job, despises working in an office, and makes less than a third of her previous income.

I take a deep breath and try to rein in my emotions before I fly off the handle. Just because we're good friends doesn't mean I'll play the part of her punching bag. She's royally pissed that she gave up doing something she loved for a boyfriend who doesn't pull his weight. I understand her frustration, but no one held a gun to her head.

This isn't the first time she's tried to shame me for something she used to do, but it will be the last.

I lift my hand to stop her from saying another word. "Hold it right there, *Saint Elsa*. Don't you dare look down your nose at me when you know you'd kill to go back to live-streaming. It's not my fault you listened to Mack and now have to work a regular nine-to-five. I love what I do and make more money than any other twenty-two-year-old I know. It satisfies my need for attention and keeps a roof over my head. If you dislike it, we don't need to be friends." My words emerge in a rush, like bullets from a machine gun aimed at Elsa's stunned face.

Elsa takes a moment to recover, taking shallow breaths as she holds back tears. Her face turn bright red as a tiny yelp escapes her lips. "I'm sorry, Vivi! You're right. I'm so pissed I shuttered my site when I was at the top of my game. I worked so hard for so long, and things were getting better. *And for what?* Mack? Now that he's more secure in our relationship, he thinks he can do whatever he wants. We hardly ever see one another. He's always out with his friends, bleeding our joint account dry." She covers her face with her hands, whimpering as she tries to shield her tears from prying eyes. It's no use. She's a mess.

"Joint account? Why on earth would you combine finances with a man who isn't your husband? Is he that good in the sack?" Now it's my turn to judge. That's a stupid move if I've ever heard one.

Elsa swipes the napkin beneath my glass and uses it to wipe her smudged mascara. "Because I'm an idiot. Because I allowed a halfway decent fuck to manipulate me into supporting him. I don't even remember the last time he made me come."

I cringe when the volume of her voice reaches the booth across the aisle, and everyone turns in our direction. Elsa doesn't seem to care. She prattles on about Mack's limp dick, lousy breath, and poor oral skills.

"I had better sex in high school, and that's saying a lot," she confesses loudly. "How the hell do I get rid of him when he won't move out?"

I slump in my seat and tell the waitress we're ready to order. This was supposed to be a casual Saturday lunch, not a political summit to discuss the state of her relationship. I'll need fuel if she wants me to contribute more than one-word replies.

"So why have you been disguising your heartache and misdirecting your anger at me?" I ask, then whisper my selection to our curious server, idling by with perked ears.

Elsa bows her head and leans forward on her elbows, her shoulders sagging with the weight of her shame. "I'm sorry. I should have listened to you. I miss my life, my platform, and, goddamn, all that money. This is my first relationship in years, and I thought he was the one. At least, I wanted him to be the one. But Mack sees me as his sugar mommy. I'm a cash cow whose milk has run dry. Every time I kick him out, he comes back and talks me into giving him another chance." She sniffles and sips her iced tea.

I'm not a Southerner. I've spent most of my life in New York and New Jersey among people who don't understand the meaning of subtle. Unlike Elsa, I don't mince words, offer passive-aggressive comments, or sugarcoat the truth. "Pack his shit, change your locks, and tell that hot policeman that lives next door, the one who's crushed on you for weeks, to spend the night."

Elsa sits back, straightening her posture as she considers my words. Her eyes grow wide as naughty thoughts of retribution float through her brain. "That's not a bad idea. He terrifies Mack."

"Bingo. Kill two birds with one stone." I nod, lean back and make room for my turkey burger and fries. "Now shut up and let me tell you about last night's fan. He was a doozy."

Chapter Three

Andrei

"I don't like this, Andrei. Our legitimate clients won't appreciate having their names entangled with someone like Volkov. It took us years and every penny we had to break away from that bastard. Once he reels us back in, he'll sink his claws deeper than before." Viktor, my middle brother and the most logical of the three of us pivots in his chair and points to his computer screen, displaying a series of encrypted emails I forwarded early this morning. He rubs his tired eyes, then adjusts his collar, fussing over a piece of lint as he complains, "I thought we agreed not to work for gangsters anymore."

"I don't think we have a choice," Vadim, my baby brother, interjects, well familiar with Boris' tactics of intimidation.

Viktor chimes in from his desk on the opposite side of the room. "We spent too many years struggling to free ourselves to get sucked in by a twenty-two-year-old bratva princess who wants to prove a point to her neglectful daddy. She isn't our problem."

"That's not fair. She's not asking to be hunted down and

Andrei is right. We still owe Volkov a favor for letting us leave." In true form, Viktor thinks only of himself and Vadim defends a woman's honor.

I probably should have consulted them before accepting the job, but you don't say no to the leader of the most brutal bratva in Brooklyn. In no way was his request posed as a question. I've known him for over twenty years, and his audacity still stuns me.

I spent the better half of last night drinking vodka and desperately trying to gather relevant information from an infuriatingly tight-lipped Boris. First, he bullies me into taking the job. Then it's like pulling teeth to make him relinquish the necessary information.

I understand his concern. He has enemies from here to Russia who would love to find and use Vivienne against him. But he came to us for a reason. Our experience and connections allow us to accomplish what he can't without sacrificing discretion or urgency.

"I didn't ask for your opinions on the matter. If I could have said no, I would have told him to go fuck himself. But I'm not taking him on over something like this. This could have gone far worse. That motherfucker could have asked me to kill someone. All he wants is to find Vivienne. We got off easy," I explain as I pour myself a glass of whiskey to soothe my nerves. My brothers rely on me to make sound decisions, and I hate letting them down. But we had no other option.

"Boris is paying the bills, but we'll run a tab and bill him at the end. Our involvement must remain untraceable not just to keep the feds off our back but also to keep his daughter safe." I bark my orders and wait for them to voice more concerns. To my surprise, they don't.

Always the multitasker, Viktor scribbles notes while he speaks. "Fine. What do we know so far?"

I return to my desk and grab my tablet, tapping my screen until I find the pitiful information I gathered last night. Groaning with exasperation and regret for dragging us into this job, I read the few facts Boris relinquished last night. "Her legal name is Vivienne Elisabeth Volkov but she may be using Vivienne Elisabeth Pinkerton, the name she had for the first year of her life, before Boris heard of her existence. Her original birth certificate didn't name a father, but Volkov officially amended those documents and she may choose a variation of that name as alias."

"I have vague memories of Charlotte. She was such a nutcase. Between her and Boris, it's no wonder this poor girl ran for her life." Vadim's snide remark rings true. It couldn't have been easy growing up with either of them.

I swipe my fingers against the screen and continue. "She's twenty-two and recently graduated from New York University. She studied marketing and mass communications. Four months ago, she emptied her bank account, deleted her social media, and fucking fell off the face of the earth. This is her most recent photo." I turn my tablet to face them and reveal the photo that's held me slightly enraptured since I encountered it late last night. Long dark hair frames her face, big blue eyes pull you in, and Cupid's bow lips leave you at a loss for words. She's become a beautiful woman—maybe the loveliest I've ever seen.

My brothers' gazes zoom in, and I can see the avarice in their pale eyes. Viktor steps closer to get a better look, nearly knocking past Vadim as he follows suit. My brothers and I share similar tastes in women, and Vivienne Volkov checks every box.

"This is Vivienne? Holy shit, she's not a little girl anymore." Vadim drools, wiping his lip as he ogles her.

"We're not starting with much. What are her likes and dislikes? Where does he believe she might have gone? Why doesn't Boris know more about his own daughter? That's despicable." Viktor licks his lips and wrenches the tablet from my hands. "How old is she again?"

"She's twenty-two, dickhead," Vadim responds with insincere judgment. He runs a hand through his auburn hair and focuses on her photo, his pupils so enlarged, his blue eyes look black. "That makes her fifteen years younger than me, eighteen years younger than you, and half Andrei's age. Besides, her father would string us up by our nuts if we touched his princess. He's probably lying and has an arranged marriage waiting for her when we bring her in."

I shake my head and tap on the screen, simultaneously disappointing them by removing the object of their fascination. "Boris doesn't plan on arranging either of his children, but he fears Charlotte might have convinced Vivienne those were his plans. He just wants evidence she's safe and a channel of communication. We don't have to return her to New York."

"And you trust him? You don't think he'll drag her back once we find her?" Vadim quirks an eyebrow.

"Boris is many things, but a liar isn't one of them." I shift my gaze to the computer monitor occupying a third of my desk and open a new case file. We have an important job, but it's not the only thing on our plate. I can delegate a few cases to our employees, but a few need to remain with the three of us. "Who wants to finish off the Donovan case? I need to devote my attention to Vivienne for the rest of the day."

"You keep Donovan. You're nearly done with that job

and diverting attention to get us up to speed with only delay its completion. I'll dive deeper into Vivienne." Vadim's emotionless voice is a dead giveaway. He wants to appear disinterested, but I see right through him.

Viktor punches his arm and grumbles through clenched teeth. "Fat chance. This is my specialty. I'll investigate Vivienne. You take the Westenra file for me, and I bet I'll find her before the end of the day."

Vadim's passive expression transforms into an angry scowl. He closes the distance between them and bumps his chest into Viktor's. "How the hell did you determine this perceived specialty? You and I do the exact same thing every day."

Accustomed to being questioned by our younger brother, Viktor pushes back. Hackles rise, and fists clench, escalating much faster than I anticipated.

"Cut it out, dickheads." I shoot out of my chair and hold my palms out, instantly annoyed that they're fighting over a woman as off-limits as Vivienne. "I said I'll look into this. If I need your help, I'll ask you for it."

They stop bickering and turn to face me, two sets of eyes narrowed in anger. "You? Why you? Don't pretend you're as tech-savvy as us." Vadim tries to shame me. He's seven years younger than me and loves making me feel like an old man.

"Because I said so." I lay down the law and expect immediate compliance. A stern gaze generally works, but I can tell by their expressions that I've failed to convince them.

"Are you hoarding her for yourself?" Viktor's accusation makes my blood boil. It's bold. Insubordinate. And absolutely accurate. But I'm forced to relent since I have no right to look and no compelling reason to keep her to myself.

"Of course not," I lie. "Take your best shots. The sooner we find her, the quicker we can close this case and get Volkov off our backs."

"Good." Vadim's wicked grin gives me pause.

"Perfect." Victor smirks but schools his features to disguise his enthusiasm.

A cold chill runs down my spine, and a sudden pang of regret fills my heart. But I shake those thoughts away and return to work, feeling confident in my ability to find Vivienne first.

In the end, this is just a job.

Chapter Four

Vadim

I was seventeen years old the first time I killed a man. The victim deserved much worse than he received, and I felt no remorse when it was done. The order came from one of Volkov's captains, who gave me the hit because he thought he could get a better deal than hiring my older brothers. That quickly changed. Within a year, I built a reputation that rivaled my brothers and settled into a fifteen-year stint that helped me accumulate a small fortune. People paid top dollar for the Balakov assassins. We were fast, discreet, and never left a trail leading back to the boss.

Do I have regrets? Plenty. I'm not a psychopath. But when you're in it, there's no room for shame or morals. I transformed myself into a cold, calculated killer out of necessity. I did what I had to do to survive. But ten years of swallowing my emotions weighed too heavily on my soul.

I had to find a way out. And I did. We did.

But the price was high, and I don't want to see us fall into that trap again.

I stare at Vivienne Volkov's photographs, the few I've found online, and feel the rare pull of desire. She was always a beautiful girl. Despite her youth, it was hard not to notice. The last time I saw her she was eighteen years old and too young to be on my radar. On one of my last jobs for Boris, he asked me to watch his house, fearing a rival was set on kidnapping his daughter. She had bodyguards surrounding her at all times, but he wanted extra protection.

I watched her come and go from the house, awestruck by the sight and inappropriately smitten. I told myself I'd wait a few years, but our split from Volkov made me abandon those prospects entirely. Pursuing his daughter would have kept me tied to his organization and I couldn't risk it.

Besides, there was a high probability Boris would have killed me for trying.

Four years later, and I have to admit, no one else has turned my head. I don't remember the last time I sought the company of a woman or spent time longing to know every-thing about her. But there was always something about Vivienne that piqued my curiosity. I often wondered if I made a mistake by not returning to Brooklyn to seek her out.

Vivienne's unconventionally beautiful with long dark hair, pale skin dotted with freckles, and sky-blue eyes too big for her face. I'm not sure why that's so appealing to me. She looks like a doll come to life, sweet and innocent, without a clue what awaits her. She's an unsuspecting lamb, unaware she's being hunted by three wolves.

She has no idea who's coming for her.

I check my messages and return a phone call to a connection in Houston. His hacking abilities are far better than mine, and although I can't give him the details about Vivienne, I ask him where's the best place to start. He offers a long list, and I spend the rest of the afternoon implementing his suggestions.

A quick call to my connection at the State Department confirms she hasn't left the country, at least not under her real name. She's obviously secured a new identity because all activity under Vivienne Volkov ceased the day she left New York. Money opens doors, and it's not unfathomable that she might have applied for a new passport under her assumed name, but I'll cross that road when I've exhausted my search in the States.

When Vivienne bolted, she emptied a checking account containing less than ten thousand, and according to Boris, she hasn't touched her trust fund since she left the city. Ten thousand dollars wouldn't take her far if she's trying to rebuild her life. I have to assume she's found employment under whatever assumed name she's using. If she's working, she must have a digital trail and the only thing left is figuring out what name she's using.

I pull a pad from my desk and scribble variations of her name, then use a facial recognition search engine to scour the internet for any sign of those baby-blue eyes. As I stare at hundreds of lookalikes, I see a photo that makes my hair stand on end. It's slightly out of focus, and for a few seconds, I'm unsure what I'm looking at.

A dark-haired woman sits scantily dressed, reclining on the arm of a couch, with a notebook in her hand. Her pink bra and panties reveal nothing more than a bikini would, but it doesn't matter. She oozes sex appeal and keeps you riveted to the screen.

Is it her? The photo doesn't have a caption, but I do a

reverse search and find a related screenshot that includes a tiny logo. I angle my head and lean in, squinting to read the blurry words. Pinky's Bedroom?

What kind of business is this?

I anxiously type the name into my keyboard, repeating the words in my mind, over and over, until I swear I hear them out loud.

"Pinky's Bedroom!" Andrei jumps out of his chair and holds his fists over his head in a pompous declaration of victory. I had a feeling he'd be the one to find her. My eldest brother is relentless and hates to be outdone by Viktor and me. He circles his desk and spins his laptop, pointing to a page on the screen. "Vivienne Volkov is living under the assumed name Genevieve Pink. And it looks like Boris' daughter has been a very naughty girl."

Viktor groans, his green eyes gleaming as he stares at his screen. "Has anyone uncovered where she's located? Today, her IP address is doing business out of Brisbane, Australia. Yesterday it was Santiago, Chile. And the day before, she was in New Orleans. It's safe to say she's using a VPN to keep her location anonymous. That's a smart move, but it creates a problem for us. It will take some time to figure out an accurate location. In the meantime, I've subscribed to Pinky's Bedroom. I might be able to learn some clues by watching her live stream or hitting her up with a direct message."

My head snaps in his direction, and Andrei's eyes narrow with justifiable suspicion. Fucking Viktor always moves with lightning speed, but if he thinks I'm letting him take the lead, he's sadly mistaken.

"Hold the fuck up, cowboy." Apparently, Andrei shares my concerns. "Boris came to me. I'll be the one to reach out to her. Not you and not Vadim." He barks out his command, confident in our compliance and utterly oblivious to the fact that we're grown men.

Who the fuck does he think he is?

Viktor lifts his hand and lets his finger hover over the Return button on his keyboard, mocking Andrei's command. "Oops." His mouth tips into a shit-eating grin as he taps the key multiple times.

"I said no," Andrei repeats his order, but it falls on deaf ears. He's our big brother, not our father.

While Andrei and Viktor argue about bullshit rules and discretion, my fingers go to work, typing furiously, setting up an account, and slyly entering payment information. I create a username but put absolutely zero creativity into it. There's no time for slick and enticing monikers like BigDickVadim or BlueEyedKiller. In a panic, I tap the Create button, and VB731 comes to life. It's essential to keep a semblance of anonymity.

"VB731? Your birthday is a dead giveaway, jackass. You think I can't see you in her room?" Andrei stops scolding Viktor and directs his disapproval at me. "There's no reason for all three of us to get involved. She's a job. Nothing more." He folds his arms across his chest and sighs, shaking his head as he storms toward his desk.

"Vivienne doesn't know who I am. If I use something like User123, she'll suspect a troll." The point is to make her comfortable enough to talk to me.

Andrei's protests aren't convincing. We have the same taste in women. If I'm smitten, so is he. And so is Viktor. I know he wants to look away. Even as I fill out my profile and wait patiently for the start of the live stream, warning sirens are sounding off in my brain.

It would be safer to pretend she's just like any other job.

Vivienne's a bratva princess, Boris Volkov's daughter, and Vasily's baby sister. Those are enough reasons to delete my account. Pursuing her isn't worth testing their patience or. mercy.

But what's the harm in taking a peek?

Chapter Five

Vivi

There's a difference between pretending and performing. Pinky is more than my alter ego. She's the person I aspire to be.

She's wild, carefree, and lives by her own rules.

She's not me—not yet.

But one day soon, art and life will meet. Vivienne and Pinky will violently crash like atoms and fuse to form something new. That day is near. There's an energy in the air, a palpable buzz filtering through my soul, urging me to take a chance and shake things up.

I've felt it before. Shortly before my move, days before all hell broke loose, my mother revealed my father's plans to marry me to a man named Alexei Grinkov. Typically, I take everything she says with a grain of salt, but I couldn't ignore the sinking feeling I got when I visited my father the next day. He was secretive, moody and refused to look me in the eyes.

I didn't want to believe it, but my intuition has rarely steered me wrong. His strange behavior made it impossible to ask him directly. If my mother was right and he knew I'd learned of his plans, he might have taken drastic measures to keep me from fleeing. I couldn't take that chance.

Leaving New York was the hardest thing I've ever done. This is the first time I've ever been on my own, paid my own bills, and made decisions without consulting my parents. My mother knows I'm safe, but I refuse to tell her where I am. I don't trust her to keep the information to herself or not to use it as a bargaining chip against my dad.

I love her, but her priorities are out of whack. She'll swear to anyone who listens that she fought to keep me safe from my crazy father but was bullied into giving me up. I was twenty when I realized her actions had nothing to do with protecting me. First, she hid me from my father as retaliation for his abandonment. She wanted to be his queen, the woman behind the powerful pakhan—cherished, spoiled, and wealthy beyond her wildest dreams. But he was tired of her antics, and her plans fell through, leaving her a bitter woman. Everything she did and put me through was done entirely for selfish reasons.

My maternal grandmother told me the truth. She said I lived a precarious existence under my mother's care. Fortunately, my circumstances improved when my father paid her enough money to start a new life in Europe. He forced my mother to give him full custody, and bought her a house in France to ensure he'd know where to find her.

I love my father, but life as the only daughter of a pakhan isn't a walk in the park. He had enemies on every street corner and feared I'd become the victim of misplaced retaliation. His overprotective nature made sense, but his fears made it impossible for me to breathe. I lived a sheltered life, smothered by the weight of my father's overzealous attempts to keep me safe. It warped my brain and made me the stir-crazy girl I am today.

I lived twenty-two years like a Russian Rapunzel, doing nothing without a gang of escorts packing enough heat to fight a war. It was claustrophobic and maddening. I spent most days choking on my tight leash, foaming at the mouth for the tiniest bit of freedom. By the time I left, I was sure I was only months from losing my mind completely.

For these reasons, I won't ever go back to the way things were. I don't care if I lose my trust fund or spend the rest of my life on the run. The only person who determines my future is me.

For once, I'll choose what I want when I want it—or I won't choose at all.

I wander into my bedroom and slide open my lingerie drawer. After four months on the job, I've acquired quite a collection. Vivienne prefers a sensible pair of cotton panties. I recently found some adorable ones that denote the days of the week. They're comfortable and nostalgic. I'm pretty sure I wore similar ones when I was a kid. Pinky likes satin and lace sheer enough to show a hint of nipple. It's best not to show too much on a live stream. If they want to see the girls in all their glory, they need to fork over five hundred dollars for a private session.

If that makes me a sex worker, then so be it. It's an honest day's work, and I have bills to pay.

The alarm on my phone chimes, and I turn my head to check the clock on my nightstand. I have fifteen minutes to doll myself up before my live stream begins. The best platforms thrive on consistency, and I've made it a point to be punctual.

Tonight, I'm reading a passage from a daddy romance, a wide-age-gap love story about a college freshman who hooks up with a man thirty years her senior. She claims to only want an experienced man to show her the ropes, hoping he'll teach her things a guy her age would know nothing about. Much to her surprise, he rocks her world and persuades her to return for more. And more. And more. Apparently, he's got great stamina for a man in his forties.

What can I say? It's a work of fiction.

I tell myself I'm playing to my audience, giving them what they want, whether I enjoy the content or not. Many of my subscribers are older men fantasizing about recapturing their youth with a much younger lover. It's important to feed that erotic escape by acting like I'm just as into it as them. That's what I told myself in the beginning. But now, I'm not so sure. Lately, I've found myself attracted to older men. Does that mean I have daddy issues? It doesn't matter. It's too close to showtime to shrink my brain with this nonsense.

The clock ticks close to seven, and these invented distractions have gotten me behind schedule. Instead of opting for the pink lace I have laid out on my bed, I lift my hair into a messy top-knot bun, remove my cotton bra and slip on a tight, cutoff shirt emblazoned with the words Baby Girl. It works with my Friday panties, and when I top off my ensemble with knee-high socks, I look like a dirty old man's dream.

This should horrify me, but like I said, image is everything. I have a part to play, and if staring at a naughty schoolgirl gets them off, who am I to judge?

Besides, behind a mask of anonymity, I'm not afraid to get in touch with my sexy side and embrace my inner tramp. God knows she's kept her cool long enough, and this is the only time I let her out to play.

I turn on my bedroom camera and adjust the ring light

toward the headboard, allowing me to recline into the pillows while I read. The first half of my story draws a crowded room of fevered followers, chiming in with comments ranging from compliments on my outfit choice to offers from potential sugar daddies. Their praise makes me nervous, but I clear my throat and continue, hoping to finish the first chapter without laughing.

A succession of pings makes my eyes drift to the tiny box notifying me of incoming private messages. The first few are the usual suspects, men who want me to finish the story topless but settle for a sheer blouse or a thin tank top that highlights my nipples. I'm not comfortable showing too much skin yet. If they want to take out their cocks and jack off while I read, they're more than welcome to pay me five hundred to feign excitement.

I scroll through the requests and spot someone new. Andrei43 appears on my screen with a slightly blurry photo, nothing more than a few words highlighting his profile and a date signifying he just subscribed today. I zoom in and make out a pair of steel blue eyes that make my heart skip a beat, but they quickly disappear into the darkness. He adjusts his posture and angles the camera to cut him off at the neck. I only caught a quick glance, but he looked older and damn good for his age. He looks familiar but I can't put my finger on who he resembles. I know it's going to bug me for the next hour. Have we met before?

His chiseled jaw poking out from the top of the screen is sprinkled with salt-and-pepper stubble, making him look powerful and distinguished, like a sexy senator or CEO. The butterflies fluttering wildly in my roiling belly make my trembling finger hover over the button before finally accepting his message.

Andrei43: Are you free to talk? I'd love to get to know more about you.

I smile at the words, unsure why I'm excited to talk to someone I've never met.

PinkysBedroom: Of course.

Chapter Six

Andrei

This is a first for me.

I stare, transfixed, at Vivienne Volkov, and my heart slams into my chest. The photos I printed from various online searches were fuzzy at best. I remember her younger version. Her beauty was obvious, but I never expected she'd transform into this level of perfection. I maximize the screen, and my jaw drops, my brain swimming with lust as I gaze at the incarnation of my teenage fantasies. Vivienne reminds me of the kind of girl I conjured in my post-pubescent mind. When I'd thumb through my father's secret stash of *Playboy* magazines, jerking off under the covers and dreaming about women who would never give me a second glance.

It's uncomfortable watching Boris' daughter flaunt her sexuality. Vivienne knows how to work the camera. While I waited for the live stream to begin, I checked out a few other sites to kill some time, and none compared to hers.

I can tell why she's so popular. It's more than her stunning beauty. She talks to her audience about silly things, what she ate, the color of her nail polish, and a little story about getting caught in the rain. By the time she settles into her bed and slides a pair of glasses on the bridge of her button nose, I'm on the edge of my seat, desperate for more.

While she reads a naughty story, my eyes focus on the shape of her mouth, glossy pink lips parting as she describes with graphic detail the love affair between an older man and his teenage daughter's best friend. Her honeyed voice spins the titillating tale and offers her audience a window into her filthy mind. I'm intrigued by the words and fascinated by the gorgeous woman reading them. Every syllable that falls off her lips has me hungry for more.

I need to remind myself this is a job. Nothing more. Watching Vivienne is simply a means to an end. While my brothers utilize covert methods to determine her location, I'm taking a more traditional path and doing my own investigation. She appears safe, and I can tell by her content that no one is coercing her to do this. She's not revealing very much skin and offers a fair disclaimer to anyone seeking a private session not to expect her to get naked. If someone else was in charge, they'd surely make her offer whatever it takes to make money.

I breathe a sigh of relief and watch the comments continue to roll in. Some perverts perform the online version of catcalling and whistling. They beg her to flash her tits or ass, and a few are brazen enough to demand a pussy shot. My hackles rise with a sense of territorial rage, as if I have a claim over a woman I've never met. I fight the urge to threaten them with a slow death and make the impulsive decision to request a private session.

I'm not alone. Vivienne or Pinky, whatever she's calling herself, has a barrage of requests, and the system automatically asks me if I want to be added to a waiting list if I'm not selected. I growl with a mix of anger and disappointment as

I click yes, still unsure if I want to call it a night or wait for her to decide which man she'll choose. She has no reason to go with a new subscriber when she could select one of her regulars.

"All right, everyone, it looks like I've got a long line of fans who want to talk to me one on one." She covers a soft giggle with her hand and shuts her notebook, placing it on the nightstand beside her. I watch her drop her hair and let the long, brown waves fall across her shoulders. She swings her legs off the bed and then stands as she waves to the camera. I lean closer, salivating at the sight of her jiggling breasts, tracing each mound with my finger as if they're the first ones I've ever seen. I don't know what has gotten into me, but for the first time in ages, it feels like I'm directing my life onto its proper course.

I must be out of my mind. She's Boris' daughter—a forbidden and unholy choice if ever there was one.

A box on the screen asks me if I'd like to turn on my camera and microphone. I panic, unsure if I should reveal who I am so soon. I wait a beat, my finger floating over my keyboard, then turn to tap the base of the lamp on my desk, darkening the room. I'm not a young man and I don't need the harsh light to make me look an old, decrepit man.

I clear my throat and click my mouse, cringing when my face appears on a smaller screen. It's a shame I didn't take time to comb my hair.

"Hello, Andrei." Vivienne offers a sweet smile and crawls onto her mattress, falling onto a pink pillow stomach first as she adjusts her view. "Is that what you'd like me to call you?"

"Andrei is perfect." My heart swells, growing exponentially with every word she utters. She's stunning. Breathtaking. A sweet, innocent morsel of subdued sexuality that needs to be unleashed.

Perhaps, I can help with that. I want to help her with that.

"That's nice. It means warrior. Are you a fighter, Andrei?" she breathes, her honeyed voice weakening my resolve.

I clear my throat and try to control the beat of my racing heart. It's useless. I'm so over the edge I may never make it back alive. "I am. I fight for the things I want. Are you really Pinky?" Of course, I know she's not, but my brain is swimming with lust and incapable of forming a suitable reply.

She hesitates, considering my question before she answers, "You can call me Vivi." Her cheeks flush, and her exuding naïveté brings my cock to life. This is a new kink. My previous girlfriends have always been a few years younger or older than me. Vivi is practically a teenager. It's obscene. Despicable. And holy fuck, it gets me so damn hot.

"Vivi? That's adorable. How old are you, sweetheart?" My lusty gaze falls on the cleavage peeking out from the top of her shirt, and I fight my desire to lean closer. Flirting online is a brand-new experience for me. I've never been good in person, but conveying my sincere interest through a computer feels impossible.

I need to win her trust but I don't want to come off as a creep.

My anxiety vanishes when she smiles, her blush deepening as she lifts her tablet above her and lies on her back. "I'm twenty-two. How about you?"

"Forty-three. Is that too old for you?" I recline in my chair and put my feet up on the desk. It's an idiotic question that she can't answer honestly if she wants to make money.

Her platform caters to men like me, older men looking for a younger submissive playmate and predators looking for easy prey. She doesn't know which category I fall into, but in her tiny pretend world, it doesn't matter.

"No," she whispers, then raises the volume of her voice. "You're an exceptionally handsome man. Are you married?"

I chuckle, amused by her question. I shake my head and undo my tie, wrapping the silk around my fist as I pull it off. Her eyes widen as she watches, her pupils overtaking her baby-blue irises. "Thank you for saying that. I think you're fucking beautiful. And no, I'm not. No wife. No girlfriend. How about you? Does your boyfriend know you do this?"

Her expression softens with my confession, and she props her tablet on a pillow, taking a moment to position it properly before answering. "I don't have a boyfriend. But if I did, of course, he would know. Secrets ruin a relationship."

"They do," I agree. "Tell me something, baby girl. Why do you do this? Is it just for the money?" I'm not a man who uses monikers, but I've spent so much time staring at her chest that it's the first thing that comes to mind. Vivienne is a fresh new book I've just cracked open, and I'm dying to read every page.

"Why do I talk to men like you?" A smile touches those pouty bee-stung lips, and my heart swells, wondering if she's sincerely flirting, and eager to listen to whatever she says. "Money is a big part of it. But I enjoy the attention."

"Did you not get enough growing up? Or did you get too much and miss it?" I soften my tone, fearing she'll consider my question an accusation or judgment.

She tenses and lifts her gaze to the ceiling, lost in thought as she considers my question. "I got enough, but it was always the wrong kind."

My brows crease with genuine curiosity. "What's the wrong kind?"

"My mother was absent and my father was overprotective. He believed the world was out to harm me. It wasn't positive attention. I crave eyes, not a prison."

Boris is notoriously protective of the ones he loves and always feared for his daughter's safety. She may have lived in the lap of luxury, but a cage is a cage, even when the bars are made of gold.

"Do you still live at home? Do they know you do this?" I hate prying so soon or playing twenty questions, but I have a job to do, and I don't want to get sidetracked by lust.

Vivienne shakes her head. "No to both. They wouldn't understand. They'll throw money at me and insist I stop. But I'm just getting started." A rush of pink stains her cheeks, and her stern voice turns silky. "What about you, Andrei?"

"Me? My father passed years ago, but my mother knows what I do."

She narrows her gaze, biting her lip to stifle a smile. "You know what I mean, mister. Tell me something about you."

"I live in New York. Where do you live?" It's an easy thing to confess. It's a city of eight million. She won't automatically believe I'm tied to her father.

She snuggles into her pillow and sinks her teeth into her bottom lip. "I make it a point not to share where I am. Someone in my position needs to be careful about attracting stalkers. Sorry." I'm happy she's cautious, but her diligence makes my job more difficult.

"Don't apologize, doll. You should take precautions. I'd kick down your door if I knew where you lived." I regret my words for a moment, but she soothes my doubts with the sexiest smile.

"Now you've made me want to tell you," she purrs, her baby-blue eyes hazy with lust.

I lean forward, lost in her beautiful face, and whisper, "Tell me what makes you feel good. How do you like to be kissed?"

"Slowly, I think," she breathes, her chest rising and falling as her pulse quickens. I can tell she's aroused. Her rosy lips and the dewy sheen of sweat on her face are tell-tale signs.

"You think? Don't you know?" I rasp, the throbbing cock in my pants making it difficult to speak.

She covers her face with her hands and giggles with embarrassment. "I haven't been kissed enough to know what I like. But I think I'd like it soft, then hard, then soft again."

My pulse kicks up. My mouth turns into the fucking Sahara. I swallow the lump in my throat and struggle to form a reply that doesn't make me sound creepy. "I'll have to remember that."

"What do you like, Andrei? What's your favorite thing to do to get in the mood?" she murmurs and runs a finger across her lips, licking them slowly as her eyes connect with mine.

"I like to watch," I blurt out the words before I have time to think about how they're perceived.

"Watch what? Do you like watching your girl with someone else? Why?" She doesn't mince words and goes right for the jugular.

"Sometimes. Primarily, I like to watch my girl get off. But not just any girl will do. I need a woman who can handle more than one man. Sometimes I want to watch, and sometimes I want to be the one fucking." The bourbon makes me bold, and I lay my kinky cards on the table.

"But why?" she asks again, unsatisfied with my reply.

"Because I want to watch you reach the height of ecstasy, writhing and moaning, your eyes locked on mine while you climax. I want you to know I'm in the palm of your hand, eager to give you more pleasure than you'll ever know," I speak slowly, enunciating every word to make sure she understands.

Boris is going to skin me alive.

Her eyes grow wide, but I'm unsure if it's horror or curiosity. "Will you let me watch you with a woman?"

"No, baby girl. I don't like being shared. I'm a possessive man and want to be with a possessive woman." I realize it doesn't make sense, but there's a method to my madness.

"How can you say you're possessive?" Vivi asks with a trace of laughter in her voice.

"Trust me, I am. My brothers are an extension of me. I'd never allow you to be with anyone else. You'd be ours. We'd be yours. No one else comes between us." My voice deepens, emphasizing the severity of my conviction.

Her long lashes flutter against her cheeks, and her voice lulls into a sleepy whisper. "Your brothers? If I was your girl, you'd share me with them?"

I answer without thinking because the words have been on the tip of my tongue all night. "It's your decision. If you only want me, then you have me. If you want one of my brothers, I'd learn to accept it. If you want all three of us, we'd pass you around, devour your pussy and claim every part of you. Have you ever been with more than one man?"

Her face pinks, and she offers a sheepish smile. "I can't say that I have."

"Tell me all about the last time a man made you climax.

Give me all the details, but don't mention his name." I think I've lost my mind and found it on the highway to hell. I'm a sick man growing more depraved by the second. Yet that knowledge does nothing to curb my appetite. Without thought or hesitation, I unzip my pants and fist my cock, pumping it slowly as I wait for her to begin.

She stretches her arms over her head, and the hem of her crop top reveals the swells of her sun-kissed breasts. It looks like my naughty girl has been sunbathing topless.

"What name should I use?"

My brow creases with curiosity. "Use Daddy. Call me Daddy." I groan, disgusted with myself but dying to hear her speak the word.

"Daddy?" Her blue eyes grow wide with curiosity. "You want me to call you Daddy? What will you call me?"

Her surprised expression makes my cock thicken. I love her naïveté, feigned or genuine, it makes me want to thoroughly corrupt her. "I'll call you my baby girl. Because that's what you are, sweetheart. Daddy wants to take care of his baby girl in every way. And as long as you do what Daddy says, he'll treat you like a fucking princess."

I'm a sick man. But goddamn, she makes me crazy.

She yawns like a kitten, pouting as she sighs, "Do you mind if I make up a story? I can't share one of my own."

"Why do you want to make it up? Are you afraid to kiss and tell?" I'm perplexed. I know fiction is typically better than reality, but she must have one that's good enough to share.

"No, that's not it. I'm a virgin, Daddy. All my stories are in my head." A tiny whimper escapes her lips, like she's afraid she's said too much, or maybe she's frustrated by her innocence. That won't be a problem for long.

The sound of her voice wrapped around the word

daddy nearly makes me come, but her confession stuns me still. I stop pumping my cock and stare at her in disbelief. "Are you lying to Daddy? How has someone as beautiful as you stayed innocent for so long?"

She shakes her head and brings one finger to her glossy lips. "Never."

I groan and push down the nasty words that want to fly out of my mouth. My heart thumps, echoing in my ears as I try to rein in my lust and fail miserably. I pump my cock and keep my grip firm as I slide my hand up and down my shaft, squeezing tightly until enough precum eases my friction. "Then make something up. Use your imagination and tell your daddy what you'd like him to do to you."

She purrs, whimpering softly as she swipes her index finger across her pouty lips and slides the digit into her mouth. "Does Daddy want me to touch myself?"

I grunt, "He does. Your daddy wants to see your pussy. But only if you want to show me. I'll understand if you're shy." The more I pump, the harder I get and the closer I get to my release. I'm not expecting her to comply, but the devil resting on my shoulder made me ask.

Vivienne's lips part with surprise. She sucks in a breath, pretending to be offended by my suggestion, then smiles. "Daddy wants to see my pussy? Does he want to see how wet he's made me? Does he want to make sure I'm fingering myself just right?"

This girl is going to be the death of me. She's a world-class tease but holy fuck, I love every word that spills from her mouth.

I nod and feel the sweat lining my brow slide down my temples. I'm so close, I don't want to stop. And I know one look at her sweet pussy could hurl me over the edge.

Her hand moves forward, momentarily blocking the

camera and sending me into a panicked frenzy. I stop jacking off, and use my clean hand to tap a few buttons on the keyboard, too afraid to ask her what she's doing. I don't want to scare her off and I don't want to make a fool of myself.

A blurry video reappears then shifts to the left while she adjusts her body into a different position. I lean closer to the screen, my eyes wide with avarice as I watch her slide her pink panties down her pale thighs, and past her knees before she kicks them away.

The focus returns just in time to give me the most amazing view of Vivi reclining into the mattress and spreading her legs. "Can you see me, Daddy?"

My mouth falls open, and the saliva pooling in my mouth dribbles down my chin. I swallow hard and rasp, "I can see you, baby girl. Are you going to give Daddy your pussy?"

I can hardly believe the words that are coming out of my mouth. It's depraved. Delusional. I don't even know where she is and I'm already making claims on her pussy.

"Yes! Daddy!" Vivienne cries through moans and arches her back, writhing against her pink blanket as her fingers work overtime on her tiny bundle of nerves.

"That's perfect, baby. Picture my tongue on your clit, licking that pink bud in tiny circles while I shove my fingers into your virgin cunt. I want to taste your cum, Vivi. Daddy needs to feed on your pussy and swallow every ounce of cum you can give him," I pant, pumping harder, fisting my shaft but never taking my eyes off the prize.

"Please put your cock inside me." She moves her finger through her glistening slit and spreads her folds apart. I release an audible gasp as my heart slams into my ribs. I can't close my eyes. With bated breath, I watch her thighs tremble and her hips levitate off the mattress. Vivienne squeezes her legs shut and twists into the bed, moaning as she pulls every bit of ecstasy from her writhing body.

I fall forward, panting, grunting, and groaning her name as a geyser of cum erupts from my savagely beaten cock and coats my fingers. I don't give a damn if she's Boris' daughter. From this day forward, Vivi is my little girl.

Chapter Seven

Vivi

"**W**hy do you look like the cat that ate the canary?" Elsa holds a baby-doll nightie against her torso and eyes herself in the mirror. It's Mack's birthday, and she's hoping make-up sex might alleviate some of their ongoing issues. She's smarter than that, but never when it comes to men. Mack is just another in a long line of men who have taken advantage of her.

"I don't know what you're talking about." I stand behind her and stare at my reflection, my face flushed with a dewy glow. Is this shame? *Arousal?* Perhaps a bit of both.

Things got out of hand two nights ago, and I'm only now recovering. It was the first time I ever let down my guard with a client. The only time I've ever been aroused by a man on the other side of the camera. We talked for hours, and I was tempted to refund some of his money, but he insisted on paying.

Does that make me a prostitute?

What was I thinking? When did I grow so bold? The temptation was too great. My lust overwhelmed me and turned me into desperate skank. Thirty minutes in, I was talking about foursomes with his younger brothers and eagerly calling him daddy, relishing how the word rolled off my tongue.

He asked me to do it, but he isn't the first man to request special names.

Typically, I ignore those demands and stick to my script. But Andrei made me break my rules with nothing more than his deep, gravelly voice. I can't believe how wet he made me. I can't believe I let him watch me come.

For heaven's sake, I gave him a close up of my pussy while I did it! What if he took a photo and uploads it to the internet? The scandal follows you everywhere. I'll never find a normal job and I can't livestream forever.

"You're doing it now, Viv. Where's your brain? You've been walking around like a zombie all morning." Elsa waves her hand across my face to snap me out of my daze. She's right to be annoyed. I've contributed almost nothing to our conversation.

"Sorry. I have sex on the brain," I confess, then cringe, knowing Elsa's not going to let a statement like that slide without any follow-up questions.

"Sex on the brain?" She snaps her head in my direction. Her lips part with surprise, and she leans closer to whisper, "Are you seeing someone? Did you finally give up your V-card?"

"No! But I think I'm smitten," I answer truthfully but hesitate to elaborate on the details of my downfall. She hates online dating and would look down her nose at me for falling for a client. It feels tawdry, filthy, and so fucking right. Why can't I stop thinking about him, longing to see him again and hear him call me his baby girl?

"With whom?" Elsa isn't going to let it go. A part of me

must have known that when I brought it up. I want to talk about Andrei. I just don't want to hear her condemnation. She'll talk me out of getting attached to a strange man online. These things never work out, especially on this type of platform. This isn't online dating. I'm a cam girl, and I'm a staunch believer in maintaining boundaries.

Last night I had a long session with Andrei's younger brother, Vadim. He asked me to keep it a secret for now and said he'd see me tonight. But I don't think he will. Only Andrei has booked a private session, and after he did, I blocked off the rest of the evening's sessions in case Andrei wanted more time.

It's not that I didn't enjoy Vadim's conversation. He's far more shy than his brother, opting to dim the lights and disguise his face like a man forced into witness protection. I'm used to it. Men don't want their families to know what they're doing and why they're spending so much money on the app.

I can't believe I was so attracted to a faceless man, but Vadim was so easy to talk to, I hardly noticed when one hour rolled into two. His sweet words and gentle nature made me instantly warm up to him. We talked, flirted, shared pet names and discussed intimate fantasies. But nothing more. I wanted to get to know him apart from his brother.

I didn't let it go as far as I wanted for fear he'd give Andrei a play by play. I know they say they share women, but I don't understand how they put that into practice. No one has explained the logistics and frankly, I'm afraid to ask.

And why do I care? How has this man crawled under my skin so fast?

"No one important. It was a chance meeting, and no one I'll ever see again." I wave her off and continue browsing through the lingerie section, looking for something special for tonight.

I'm not being cagey. Eventually, I'll need to confess for the sake of my sanity, but there's no sense in mentioning a man I'll never meet. Besides, I think it's best to maintain an air of mystery around what I do. Elsa worked CamLife for over a year, but the only thing she ever exposed was her feet. I may not get naked, but I reveal much more than my toes.

"It sounds important, or you wouldn't have brought it up. Next time you see him, introduce yourself and tell him you're available. Believe me, he won't turn you down. You're gorgeous and too sweet for your own good. Guys eat that shit up." Elsa leads us toward the cashier's box and continues lecturing me, "It's about time you have a real face-to-face relationship and stop spending so much time talking to men online."

Her words deflate me. She's right. Andrei and Vadim's level of attention is nothing new. Most evenings, I speak to three or four guys, and it's my job to make them feel special. I flirt with all of them because that keeps them returning for more. It's not always easy to pretend to be interested, but I try my best because it's all part of the fantasy I'm trying to create. If these guys wanted reality, they'd stick to the real world and save themselves five hundred bucks.

But I didn't need to pretend with Andrei *or Vadim*. They brought that side out of me out without trying. Imagining them together got me so aroused I had to rein in my emotions before I said or did anything I'd regret. Although looking back, we've crossed more than a few lines.

"You're right. I need to live more. I should have experiences offline with real men who have six-pack abs, chiseled jaws, and sexy voices that make me weak in the knees." I imagine Andrei's smoldering blue eyes, and Vadim's hot body—the one he revealed after he removed his dress shirt to jack off to one of my stories—and sigh. With a flushed face and tight voice, I inadvertently describe them to a tee.

"That's a tall order, sister. But you may want to add a massive penis if you're already creating a fictional man. Have you seen one yet?" Elsa never lets me forget that tiny detail. I regret telling her about my lack of experience. I was looking for guidance, not providing ammo for constant mockery.

Technically, I haven't. Neither man revealed anything below the waist but simply described what they did in detail. And even if they had shown me the goods, I still don't think I could characterize that as having seen a cock in the flesh.

"I know what a cock looks like, for heaven's sake. But no, I have yet to hold one in my hand. Obviously, I'm not a Goody Two-shoes. I'm open to the experience when the right opportunity presents itself. I didn't grow up like you. Your mom gave you the freedom to date and meet boys. My father was strict, and his constant supervision made it hard to run around New York grabbing penises left and right." The last words emerge louder than I intended, and the woman beside me gasps with horror.

"Settle down, Karen," Elsa huffs and pulls me closer, eyeing the older woman with derision. "She said she *did not* grab penises. Besides, she used the scientific term, which makes this a discussion about biology, not sex. Beat it." She hands the saleswoman her credit card and helps me place my items on the counter.

"Thanks, girl. I'm positive I'm going overboard, but I'm pretty sure all this crap is a work-related tax deduction." I make excuses, hoping she doesn't notice the crotchless panties in the mix. Why would I buy such a thing? I would never show my pussy on camera. *Or would I?* I smile, imagining what position would show me in the best light before mortification washes those thoughts away. I don't even remember the last time I waxed.

"Are we still on for lunch, or must you return to your cameras?" Elsa leads us down the escalator, through the glass doors, and onto the sidewalk. I check the time on my phone and notice an incoming message from the CamLife app.

> VB731: Can I see you again tonight? I noticed you blocked off a stretch of hours.

I stare at the message and consider logging off. It's not the first one I've received today. After Andrei confirmed his appointment, I disabled the option for anyone to book after 8:00. He wants to apologize for disappearing for a day, but swore he was unable to book yesterday. That was entirely my doing. I needed time to analyze the unfamiliar emotions warping my brain.

Besides, I'm exhausted. Business is booming and wearing me out.

I should take a break from work and cool these flirtations before they get out of hand. I can't fall for strangers. No one is ever what they appear to be online, and I know better than anyone that these guys are almost always married.

It's a recipe for disaster, but these justifiable concerns do nothing to deter me. There's something about them. Something different I want, need, and can't do without. Call it intuition or curiosity, but a nervous tingle in the pit of my stomach makes me hit the Reply button.

PinkysBedroom: I'm seeing your brother at 7. But I have an opening at 8:30.

I tap the Send button and wait for him to answer. I can't let fear of attachment get in the way of doing my job. My rent won't pay itself, and hell will freeze over before I tap into my trust fund. That's a surefire way to get my dad and his bully soldiers on the first plane to New Orleans to drag me home.

VB731: I snagged that spot and I can't wait to see you, little girl.

Butterflies flutter. My heart pounds. His pet name thrills me, and I envision another night with another dominant man who wants me to call him Daddy.

Maybe I've uncovered my kink.

Chapter Eight

Andrei

"**H**ey, sweetheart. How is Saturday treating you?" I drop my voice an octave and let the words roll off my tongue like honey. I'm not sure it sounds natural, but I try my best to appear smooth. I feel like an amateur, but I really want her to like me.

"Hi, Daddy." Vivienne chews her lips, batting her lashes as she purrs. "Saturday just got better now that you're here." She appears on the screen and steals the breath straight from my lungs.

I clench my jaw to keep it from falling to the floor and stare helplessly at the most beautiful woman I've ever seen. For a moment, I consider keeping her all to myself, but the two grown men hovering in my periphery guarantee there's little hope of seeing that through.

"You're a little adorable," I gush like a teenage boy but hide my smile from my brothers loitering nearby. They don't need to know this is far more than a job. I'm supposed to be the levelheaded one who takes care of business without letting emotions cloud my judgment.

And I'm failing miserably.

"How was your day? Did you think about me?" Vivi whispers sweetly, and I'm instantly aroused by the soft lilt of her voice. My heart skips a beat, and she pulls me into her world with nothing more than a shy smile.

She's lying in bed, on her side, leaning on her elbow. The room is dimmed and bathed in rose-colored light to cast her in a flattering light or make her viewers believe they're peeking into a teenage girl's room. She succeeds flawlessly. I'm almost ashamed to stare.

I nod, lost in a daze, as my hungry eyes devour every inch visible through my small screen. "I don't think I've stopped thinking of you all day, little girl."

Behind me, out of sight from the camera, Viktor pours himself a glass of bourbon and glares at my computer, gesturing to our younger brother to pull up a chair in the camera's blind spot.

They don't need to supervise. I'm more than capable of getting the job done.

"What did you think about? Did my story give you nasty dreams?" Her wide eyes narrow with suspicion, then a slight smile touches her lips. She laughs, daring me to reveal my wicked thoughts.

"You don't need to speak a word to give me filthy dreams. What you did, what we did, was enough to get me off for the rest of my life. But yes, your stories help." I'm out of my element, but the faster I win her trust, the sooner I can pry the information we need. I'm not necessarily impatient. These things take time. But it's crucial to move this along before my feelings throw me off course.

Last time, I spent three fucking hours flirting, laughing, and jacking off, yet failed in my one objective to find out where the hell she lives. That's why my brothers chosen to stand by and observe. They suspect I'm too infatuated to trick her into revealing her location and plan to take over if I fail.

And maybe they're right.

I'm better than this. I spent years making people talk, discovering their weaknesses, and manipulating them into providing valuable information they swore they'd keep to their graves. Pulling a con is serious work, and that's precisely what this is. I need to convince Vivienne to provide information she's fervently guarding and I'm beginning to doubt that day will come.

Perhaps, I'm dragging this out because I want to figure out why I count the minutes until I see her face again. My heart aches to touch her. My soul longs to hold her in my arms and make her feel safe. Her father is the most dangerous man I know, and he's expecting us to bring her home. The sooner we learn her location, the faster we can hop on a plane and get her back to New York. When that happens, Vivienne Volkov officially becomes off-limits.

"Do you want to listen to another story? I have a few you haven't heard before." Vivi lifts a pink notebook covered with tiny daisies and flips through it, scanning the pages before she continues. "I have one about a knight and a damsel in distress. And an over-the-top spicy alien romance."

"As much as I love your dirty books, I'd rather hear more about my girl," I say, hoping she opens up about her life. I don't know if our playful banter is genuine or if she excels in stringing men along. It's an excellent skill for someone in her position, and I can't blame her for using it.

She's better at it than me. Ever since she came into my life, I can hardly tie two sentences together.

Charisma comes with experience, and I've always been fortunate to attract the opposite sex without trying. That's not a brag or flex. I don't seek attention because I'm too busy growing our business to nurture a relationship worth building.

"What do you want to know?" Vivienne smiles, and her tense body relaxes into a fuzzy pink pillow. "I'm 5'3. You know I have brown hair and blue eyes. No pets, but I love cats. I haven't decided what kind of job I want to do full time or where I want to put down roots. And you apparently know exactly what to say to convince me to remove my panties." She sinks her teeth into her bottom lip and provides details I don't want my brothers to hear.

"I'm sure you'll figure it out soon." I take a sip of bourbon and clench my jaw, the strong aroma biting at my taste buds. "Tell me something, angel. Have you ever met someone from this platform in person?"

Vivi shakes her head. "No, but lately, I've been tempted. I've had an interesting two days."

Vadim steps closer, wanting to reveal his presence to the object of his newfound affection. He's made it clear he's smitten, but I've asked him to hang back until we learn more about her location. I wave him off, gesturing for him to return to his place in the camera's blind spot, and he reluctantly returns, murmuring profanities under his breath.

I don't want her to believe I had others watching the other night. It would be another betrayal of trust.

I may not be able to confess I'm working for her father, but I'll be damned if I let someone see her pussy without her permission.

"Does that include me?" I'm not a flirt, but Vivienne makes it easy to turn on the charm. She's so young, beautiful, and brimming with sexual curiosity. It's fucking intoxicating.

"Maybe," she gushes, giggling sweetly as she rolls to

her side. In my periphery, Vadim's tight lips curve in a silly grin as he watches her gather her hair into a messy bun. He claims they haven't met, but he looks hopelessly smitten. I have a nagging suspicion that he's withholding information.

We're nowhere closer than where we started. While Viktor twiddles his thumbs, complaining about our lack of progress while doing nothing to help, Vadim and I have been on his computer most of the day, working behind the scenes with various connections to pinpoint her precise location. We haven't gotten far, but at least we're trying.

"What did you do today, darling?" I'm only mildly curious. I want to ask far more critical questions than her daily whereabouts, but I can't neglect my obligation. We've gotten nowhere searching for her digital footprint. CamLife encrypts their information for the sake of privacy. We only found her photo online because someone took a pixelated screenshot.

That's why I need to search for clues in her conversation. Little things can give it away—a restaurant, mall, or place of business. Getting her to talk about them will help our investigation.

Vivi pauses to consider the question and lifts her hand, waving her manicured fingers. "I got my nails done. Do you like it?"

"I do. That's a lovely shade of pink." I can see why her nickname is Pinky. Everything about this girl is pink. Typically, I'd find it irritating, but she's so adorable it fits. "What else?"

"I went shopping and had lunch downtown," her voice drops to a purr, and she tangles a finger through her long, brown hair. She makes it so easy to fall under her spell, but I need to rein in my traitorous heart and stick to business.

Asking her to elaborate will only make me look suspicious, but I try, nonetheless. "What did you eat?"

Vivienne shakes her head and makes a face. "I have terrible self-control. After a long day of shopping, I ate a burger, fries and shared a milkshake." A crimson flush spreads from her chest to her face, as if her appetite is something to be ashamed of.

I nip that crazy shit in the bud. "Next time, get your own shake. You're a growing girl who needs her sustenance to keep looking as fine as you do."

She covers her smile with her hand, and her bright eyes gleam with appreciation. "You're a sweetie, Andrei. What brings you here for a second night? Someone as handsome as you should be breaking hearts."

"I'm here because I want to be here." I tense, fearing my emotions are too easy to read.

Vivi closes her eyes and hugs her pillow, smiling as she sighs. "I'm glad you're here, too."

I know nothing about her audience or the kind of men who come here. Until recently, I didn't know these kinds of things existed. But if she's implying I'm lonely, then she's half right. I've never had any trouble finding companions. I just wish I could meet someone who motivated me to stick around.

"What did you buy yourself? I hope it was something nice." I change the subject, hoping to jump back on track before I forget why I'm here. It's so easy to slip away into a fantasy world, believing she shares my attraction, but the odds are she's playing me for a fool or simply experimenting with her sexuality. I doubt she'd want to hitch her wagon to a man only a few years younger than her father. Especially one she met online.

For the sake of Boris and our business, I return to my

task and try to wrangle the name of a local store. I've wasted too much time with my head in the clouds.

Vivienne is a job. Nothing more.

I repeat those words in my mind, hoping to convince myself they're true.

"Let me show you what I bought," she squeals and pans the camera to the right, wiggling her behind to show me the pink baby doll panties decked with rows of lace across her round ass. My mouth waters at the glorious sight, and my stiff cock rams into my zipper. She really knows how to pull out the big guns. No wonder she's so popular.

Vadim groans, quickly emptying his drink before pouring himself and Viktor another. He shakes his head and clenches his fist, his stern gaze shooting daggers into my heart.

My brothers and I are close. We're more than family. We're best friends who spend most of our time together. From the outside looking in, I have no doubt it appears unhealthy. Viktor and I are in our forties, and Vadim is nearly there. We should have wives and families of our own, but none of us have ever come close.

We're notoriously horrible at relationships and typically find amusement in quick and easy encounters that finish long before they get off the ground. Who has time to fall in love when we run a multi-billion-dollar business and insist on doing most of the work ourselves?

"Those are some hot fucking panties," I grunt, biting my lip to stifle the growl vibrating in my chest.

"I'm glad you like them. I thought about you and your brothers while I was shopping. Maybe you can tell them all about them." Her sultry voice makes my heart pound like a jackhammer, and I lean in, salivating, with wide eyes before she readjusts the camera and angles it back to her gorgeous face.

"I will," I whisper, mindful that my brothers are sitting nearby, listening to every word. The thought of watching her with them, letting me direct her, her eyes fixed on mine while she climbs the height of ecstasy, pulls a low growl from my throat.

An easy smile plays on the corners of her mouth, and I nervously moisten my dry lips, eagerly awaiting her following words. "You said you'd share me with them," she murmurs, pausing to form words she doesn't appear comfortable repeating. "What does that mean? Do you take turns? Would you take me at the same time? Do you watch everything?" Vivienne rests her head on her pillow and stares at the camera, her lashes fluttering as she takes a deep breath.

To my right, Vadim runs his hand through his hair, pulling it hard as he stares longingly at the girl slowly stealing my heart. Viktor nods, clenching his fists as he struggles to hide his feelings. Unfortunately for him, I see right through him.

I swallow hard and clear the emotion clogging my throat. "All of the above. Like I said, I love to watch. But that's not all I want to do to you."

"What do you want—" She cuts her words and exhales, choosing not to utter the question she's dying to ask.

"I want to do everything, Vivi. *Fucking everything*."

Vivienne's expression grows pensive, her eyes drawn to something in the distance as she takes everything in. Her attention returns when a box appears on the screen and alerts us our time is almost up. She taps the screen, activating the tiny clock that counts our last thirty seconds.

"Our time is up, Andrei. It was nice chatting with you. Maybe we'll talk again soon."

I panic and search the screen for a way to extend our session. When I can't find that option, I ask her for help. "I don't want this to end yet."

Vivienne brushes away the tendrils of dark hair on her brow and shakes her head with a smile. "Sorry. The next hour is booked, but we'll chat soon. Tell your brothers I said hello." She blows a kiss at the screen and disappears with a click.

My heart plummets, and I tap my keyboard, hoping she hasn't exited entirely. It's no use. She's gone, and I'll have to wait another day to finish what we started. Not only have I failed to learn her location, but I may have frightened her away.

Loitering a few feet away, Viktor mocks me with laughter. He stands and crosses the room to grab another drink. "I thought you were on top of this? You still haven't come closer to finding out where she lives."

My hackles rise, and I close my laptop, annoyed with myself, furious with Viktor, and suddenly aware that Vadim is no longer in the room. "Where the fuck did he go?"

Chapter Nine

Vivi

I lie in bed, my hand under my cheek and my body curled like a cat as I gaze at the screen. A man with gray-blue eyes visible through a sliver a light streaming in from another room lies on his side, his auburn hair disheveled as he tells me about his day. He's either gotten careless or grown comfortable showing his face.

"Tell me about a place you want to visit and what you'll do when you get there." Andrei's younger brother keeps his voice calm and his smoldering gaze fixed on me. He's handsome beyond words and has my undivided attention.

My hour with Andrei left me unsettled. Not because he said anything wrong. On the contrary, I half expected him to continue what began two days ago. I'd thought about it all day. I fantasized what he would say and do, but instead of kindling the fire that he ignited our first night together, he seemed far more interested in getting to know me.

I can't allow myself to fall for him. I won't let my lust transform to genuine affection. What good would that do? We'll never meet and never see this through. However much his words intrigued me, I couldn't wait to leave the call for fear I was getting in far over my head.

As much as I'd like to pretend otherwise, I'm not entirely comfortable with my sexuality, yet Andrei makes me want to explore every kink that enters my mind. If the time hadn't expired, I might have done something I'd regret. Again.

Vadim is different. I like him. I genuinely like him.

Andrei makes me feel beautiful and sexy. Vadim warms my heart and makes me feel seen. I want to meet him in the flesh, hold his hand, walk through Jackson Square, and get coffee and beignets at Café Du Monde. If I met him on a crowded street, I'd jump into his arms and beg for his love. Then I'd take him home and ride him until one of us passes out.

I lean back against my headboard and hold a pillow between my legs, clenching my thighs as I stare at the gorgeous man on my screen. While I consider his words, my eyes land on his chiseled face, auburn hair, high cheekbones, and the intricate, ornate ink peeking out from his starched collar. He's elegant and rugged, dangerous and debonair. Every time I'm in his presence, I can hardly remember anyone else.

"My father took me to Paris to meet his eccentric sister when I was seven, and I haven't been back since. I'd like to go back with someone I love, walk the cobblestone streets, watch the Eiffel Tower light up at night, and eat loads of fabulous French food," I mutter, uncomfortable providing specifics about my family life to a stranger but longing to share more of who I am with this beautiful man.

"I love Paris. Maybe we'll go together one day." His kind smile makes my heart flutter faster than butterfly wings. He unfastens his watch and unbuttons his dress shirt, pulling it off his arms to get more comfortable in bed. I stare dumb-struck at the curve of his sculpted arms and lean in, strug-gling to read the tattoos etched into his skin. I can't bear to look away.

"Maybe," I bring my hands to my hot cheeks, my brain spiraling out of control as I surrender all sanity to this hot man who has my number. How can I become aroused by two separate men, hours apart?

"What's your favorite place there?" I ask.

"I love wandering through the Tuileries Garden in autumn when the leaves have turned and the air is crisp. We'll walk from the Louvre, hand in hand, toward the Concorde, and if you're in the mood, take a ride on the Great Ferris Wheel." He's magnificent. Every word he speaks feels like it's been pulled from a dream.

Be still my heart.

"Where do you call home?" I say the words without thinking, then quickly backtrack, afraid he'll reveal his loca-tion and ask for mine. Andrei has asked this question count-less times in multiple ways and I haven't fallen for it yet. I understand the curiosity but I can't forget my father is searching for me. "No, don't answer that. It's best to keep personal details to ourselves."

Vadim chuckles and rests his head on his pillow, folding his sinewy forearms beneath his chin. "My brothers and I live in side-by-side penthouse apartments on the Upper West Side. Are you afraid I'll track you down somewhere in the city? You are a New Yorker, aren't you? I can tell by your accent."

I slap my hand over my mouth, unaware my accent was thick enough to give me away. "I grew up in Manhattan," I giggle through my fingers and confess what I can. "But I don't live there anymore. You'd have to travel a long way to run into me in my city."

"How far? How could you move away from the greatest city on earth? You must miss it," he says, his eyes bright with curiosity.

I curl into my down comforter, feeling more comfortable as the minutes tick by. "Pretty far. And yes, I do miss it. But I had to get away from my family. They interfere too much in my life."

I groan, instantly regretting bringing up my parents, but he caught me off guard. Vadim has a strange effect on me. I've abandoned all reason and jumped into the deep end of madness. I know better than this. I don't know where these men came from, and although my instincts tell me they're not connected to my father, I can't be so sure.

My safety depends on discretion.

"Are you angry with them?" Of course, he asks. I put it out there, and he was bound to bite. Maybe I want to talk about it. Perhaps it's easier to vent to a stranger who has nothing to gain or lose by knowing my business.

"It's a boring story and not worth repeating," I deflect and hope he drops it. The way he's looking at me, he could make me confess nuclear secrets.

"I understand if it's painful. But nothing you say would bore me. I want to know everything about you—whatever you're comfortable sharing." His warm tone and kind eyes tempt me to reveal the horrible truth, but I alter the facts, opting to tell him my father and I had a difference of opinion on how I should live my life. That's not entirely untrue. Not wanting to marry a man I don't love is a huge difference of opinion.

"Does he know you do this? Is that why he's upset?" he asks, and I immediately shake my head, horrified by the thought he should ever find out. I'm not ashamed of what I do, but it's not something I need to share with my father.

"No, it has nothing to do with this. And it's none of his business what I do for a living." I bring my hands to my hot cheeks and duck my head, uncomfortable with the intensity of his gaze. Maybe he still believes I can't see him.

Struggling to speak, I swallow hard and change trajectories. I take a sip of wine, counting on a surge of liquid courage to calm my nerves, then murmur, "May I ask you a question?" My voice trembles with anxiety, unsure if he'll answer truthfully.

"Do your brothers know you're talking to me?" I'm genuinely curious about how deep their connection goes. In my world, men are possessive and territorial with their women. They don't share. They wouldn't entertain the idea, let alone the execution.

He shakes his head and brings a glass of amber liquid to his lips, savoring the taste before placing it on his nightstand. His gray eyes find mine, and a faint light twinkles in their depths. "They don't. I didn't mention it. But of course, I'll tell them tomorrow."

"There are so many women on this platform. Beautiful and more experienced women who would love to be shared by three handsome brothers. Why are you wasting your time with me? You've got fantasies I'm not sure I can fulfill." I clasp my hands, wringing them tightly as I consider meeting the brothers together.

As much as I want to feign innocence, I watched hundreds of adult films before I settled on a few fantasies that piqued my nasty curiosity. And one of those included multiple men. Reality never trumps fantasy, and I'd rather not mention it to him for the sake of privacy. True fantasies, the ones that keep me up at night, are not something I want to share so soon. Even with men as handsome as Vadim and Andrei. I'm beginning to wonder what brother number three looks like.

Could they genuinely handle sharing a woman they love, or would they make me choose?

What if I can't decide?

"You haven't wasted a minute of my time. There's a reason we're drawn to you. You've got something special. Don't you feel special? You should feel like a fucking princess. And we're the three knights who climb the tower, slay the dragon, and carry you away to do dirty things." His husky voice and piercing gaze unravels my resolve.

My heart explodes, and my face grows as hot as my core.

"Where are you, sweetheart? Maybe one day we'll find ourselves in the same city and run into one another on a busy street," he rasps, his low honeyed voice stoking a gentle flame in the pit of my stomach.

The clock on the corner of the screen chimes, and I take a hard look at the man on the screen, lost in his gaze and overwhelmed by my newfound attraction to these men —brothers.

What have I become?

"Goodnight, baby. I'll send you a message on the app to make sure you don't forget about me," he whispers and mumbles something I can't understand. With ten seconds on the clock, I can't ask him to repeat it.

I wave my fingers and blow him a kiss, exhaling sharply as I pull the tank top over my head and reveal my breasts. This isn't the most skin I've ever shown, but it's the first time I've flashed my tits. His gaze sharpens and I place the tips of my fingers over my taut nipples and shield them from view. I want him to see me, but I'm not used to flaunting so much.

Says the woman who let a strange man watch her masturbate.

My loss of inhibitions has nothing to do with making money. I want him to return because I want to see him again. Not because I want another five-hundred dollars.

"I want to see you again. Message me when you have time to talk." I don't know what I'm doing, but for once I'm taking a chance and following my heart. I just hope it doesn't come back to bite me in the ass.

His eyes grow wide, his lips part to speak, and a moment later, the screen fades to black.

Chapter Ten

Viktor

"What time do we arrive?" I groan through clenched teeth, my throat too clogged with emotion to finish my thought. I'm fidgeting, adjusting my chair, fastening and unfastening my cufflinks, and wondering how the hell I'll get through this flight.

I should have stayed home. Nothing good can come from three men falling in love with the same woman. Andrei and Vadim are playing with fire. We're not prepared to share Vivienne.

Love changes everything.

A part of me regrets becoming involved in this job. I should have trusted my instincts, focused on the Donovan case, and left Vivi for my brothers. My fucking ego made me cave.

Andrei threw down the gauntlet. He challenged me and then accused me of dawdling while he and Vadim did all the work. But he was wrong. I didn't need to spend hours flirting, allowing her to tease me into a lusty frenzy to learn secrets she didn't want to reveal.

What were they thinking? Why would she tell us on her

own? She's running from her father, a man with brutal men at his disposal. Of course, she's worried for her safety.

Instead of going the traditional route of tricking her into confessing where she lives, I spent my time tracking her digital footprint. Although her VPN changed her location every time she logged in, I noticed New Orleans had an unusually high recurrence.

As soon as I learned a Genevieve Pink was living in New Orleans, I put things in motion with one of my favorite private investigators, Paul Leroy. He's relentless and a long-time resident of the city—he could find his way around blindfolded. We may have technology he could never afford, but we can't replace good, old-fashioned detective work in situations like this.

Paul found her two nights ago, probably around the same time Vadim told me he was talking with her, too—a tidbit he accidentally shared with me after consuming too much vodka. He's always been annoyingly tight-lipped, but something about her made him unload details I didn't care to hear.

Seconds after his confession, Vadim caught his mistake and asked me not to tell Andrei. I don't blame him for keeping that part a secret. Our older brother hasn't been himself. His territorial instincts have betrayed his typically stoic demeanor, and it's become evident that he wants to do something about it.

Vivienne lives in a gated community near Magazine Street in the city's Garden District. It's a nice area, relatively safe for a young woman living alone. I had her address for thirty-six hours before I shared the information with my brothers.

I'm not sure why I chose to keep it to myself. Maybe I'm just a greedy, jealous bastard who wanted to be the first to see her in the flesh. I hacked into CCTV cameras along her street, watching her as she left her apartment, then tapped into cameras on her walk into the French Quarter. I sat for hours, yearning to touch and talk to her, wondering how I fell so fast for a woman I'd never met.

"How did you manage to find her first? Vadim and I tried for days," Andrei rants, annoyed and dumbfounded that I could beat him to the punch. He wrongly assumed he'd sweep her off her feet and make her spill the details. He's always had a way with women but didn't even come close to making her give up her location.

"Apparently, you've underestimated your brother's skills. I accomplished in two hours what you both failed to do over the course of days," I brag, inadvertently outing Vadim's secret. It was all going to come out anyway.

"Both of us?" Andre looks at Vadim, but Vadim ignores him and continues typing on his keyboard, his shoulders slumped forward as he stares at the screen. He's been communicating nonstop with my detective since we boarded our private jet, determined to track her movements until we arrive.

"It's not a big deal. I spoke to Vivienne twice. She knows I'm your brother, but I asked her not to tell you," Vadim admits his ruse without batting an eyelash. His lack of shame makes it impossible for Andrei to guilt him.

"We land in approximately forty-five minutes," a flight attendant updates us, and asks if we'd like another drink before landing.

"Good, I look forward to getting this deal closed," I lie through my teeth, then ask the flight attendant to bring me another whiskey, hoping to drown the thoughts floating around my head. I'm not the kind of guy who mixes business with pleasure, and I've tried hard to keep my distance from this assignment. But the minute I saw her photograph on Andrei's tablet, I knew I'd ultimately fail.

Nothing is set in stone. There's a possibility that I'll feel nothing when we meet.

I'm a voyeur. Of course, I was turned on by the kittenish look of her online persona. She's the most beautiful woman I've ever seen. And it was easy to get swept away by the fantasy of finding a woman we could love together. As much as we've thought about it in the past, this is the first time my brothers have tried to woo the same woman with a greater objective than simply bedding her. But something about this feels wrong. It's one thing to share a woman for one night. I'm not sure I want to do it forever.

"It may have started as an assignment, but it's become so much more. And I know I'm not alone in this," Vadim speaks up, his eyes darting back and forth from Andrei to me. "Tell me I'm wrong."

I take a sip and release a shaky breath. There's no sense in thinking too hard about something that will never happen. Things will undoubtedly change. She's too young and forbidden to pursue romantically, and I'm not interested in making her father my enemy.

"Don't bring me into this." I shake my head and deny my burgeoning fascination. It's easier to continue the charade and feign indifference than admit I can't stop thinking about her.

"No one believes you, Viktor." Andrei strides toward the back of the plane, his long legs making quick work of the short journey. He shrugs his jacket off and tosses it on the back of a chair before landing on the leather sofa. He runs his hand through his hair, tousling his salt-and-pepper locks as he huffs. "I know you're lying, and I bet if I checked your computer, I'd find Pinky's Bedroom bookmarked and saved to your favorites."

He's right. He would.

But I'm not about to admit it now.

"You two need to get your head out of the clouds. We have to be on the same page and ensure our focus is clear. We'll track her down, take her under cover of night, fly back to New York, and deliver her to her father. When all is done, we'll wash our hands and move on to the next assignment." I seethe, furious that I can't control my emotions. She's a pretty girl. Of course, I'm attracted to her. Once we've completed this assignment, these feelings will surely go away as quickly as they appeared.

As much as I want them to believe I'm unaffected by Vivi's charm, my commands fall flat. I'd love to pretend she's just another girl, like the many who have walked in and out of our lives. But I know she's not.

Holy fuck. Why does this have to be so complicated?

"Boris doesn't need to know our timeline," Vadim interjects, too consumed with his search to look up from his computer. "He trusts us to do a job and won't ask any questions if we take a few days to ensure she's safe. If you recall, Boris is not asking us to return her to New York. He just wants to know she's safe. And I'm sure he wants us to convince her to call him."

"We can't move too quickly. We need time to explore the feelings that I'm almost certain we all share. Or we might live to regret it," Andrei voices his opinion, certain we're all on the same page.

They're wrong. We don't need to explore our feelings for Vivienne. The more time we spend with her, the harder it will be to let her go.

Chapter Eleven

Vivi

"I've got fresh tea straight from the kettle," Elsa hums, her enthusiasm at an all-time high. This is the first time I've seen her all week, which isn't typical of our friendship. I assumed she'd finally given her pathetic boyfriend the brush off and had chosen to lay low while she worked through her grief. But the smile on her face doesn't exactly scream breakup.

I look around the near-empty coffee house, eyeing the two steaming cups of coffee our server set down moments ago, and stare perplexed. "Did you want tea? I could have sworn I heard you ask for coffee. Tell the server to correct it. He's a nice guy, and the place is dead. I doubt it will be a problem."

Elsa angles her head, her brows knit with confusion. She emits an audible sigh and shakes her head with exasperation. "What's going on with you? I've *got* tea. Tea! National Enquirer quality gossip!" Her high-pitched shriek makes me jump in my seat, and a few drops of coffee land on my sweater. Thank goodness I wore black. I place the cup onto the saucer and wipe my chin with a branded napkin.

"For heaven's sake. Pardon me for not automatically getting the reference. I'm from New York," I reply. "Next time, tell me you've got dirt."

She sips her coffee, wrinkles her nose with distaste, then stirs another teaspoon of sugar into the cup. "Genevieve Pink, are you seeing someone? You've been acting so mysterious the last week. Either you're hiding from the law, or you've fallen in love with a wildly inappropriate man you refuse to discuss." Elsa unbelievably hits the nail on the head. I'm not running from the law, but my father's minions are far worse.

"I have a lot on my mind." I hesitate for a moment, still unaccustomed to being called Genevieve. The only reason I chose that moniker is to make it easy for someone to call me Vivi. I should have stuck to Vivienne.

"Like what?" Elsa never lets me get away with anything. And as much as I'd love to discuss my infatuation with two, maybe three men, I'm not ready to hear her questions or condemnation. Besides, there's no way to accurately describe my feelings because I don't understand my emotions. I feel hot, bothered, and horny, but I'm unsure who I want more.

Three men are not a possibility. I don't care what they say or do with other women. I'm unsure where I'd find the stamina if I wasn't morally opposed. There aren't enough B-12 vitamins to produce the energy level I'd need to fuck three hot men on a regular basis.

Last night, the storm brewing in my panties took an exciting turn. I think I met brother number three. When I subtly asked if his brothers used the app, he ignored my question. I wanted to try a bolder approach, but asking a man about other men when they're paying five hundred dollars for an hour of your time is bad for business.

His name is Viktor. He's broad-shouldered, barrel-chested, tatted, rippled with dark-blond hair and striking green eyes. He looks like he's been torn from the pages of a romance book cover—the wild ones that keep me up way past my bedtime. There was no reason a man who looked like him should be searching for a good time online, but I could say the same for Andrei and Vadim.

Each one is a magnificent specimen of masculinity, and responsible for turning me into a needy puddle of lust every time we talk.

"Are you listening to my story? I never have good tea, and you're acting like you don't want to hear it," Elsa whines loudly enough to snap me out of my lusty daze. I'd almost forgotten she was here.

"No, sorry, I'm so distracted. I had a long night. Spill your tea. I'm listening." I'm failing as a friend. Elsa might have her faults, but she's always been there when I needed her.

After four months on the run, looking over my shoulder and hiding from my powerful father, I've become self-absorbed and wary of strangers. I work so hard hustling online, making connections, and bringing in new customers, I hardly have a chance to experience anything in the real world. Elsa is the exception, and I'm grateful for her patience.

Our friendship keeps me sane.

Elsa gives me a broad smile and jazz hands, leaning forward to speak as if someone is idling nearby. The coffee house is a ghost town. "I took your advice." Her first sentence is short, sweet, and utterly vague. I can tell by the gleaming look in her eyes that she wants to draw it out over the next hour.

I get it. Today is dedicated to Elsa, and I'm here to provide feedback.

"My advice? What did I suggest?" I break a piece of biscotti in half, tap out the crumbs on a napkin, take a bite, and continue, "Don't keep me waiting. I'm all ears."

Elsa takes a deep breath, filling her lungs to ensure she can get through the following sentence without a break. She wiggles her bottom and scoots to the edge of her seat. "Do you know there's a sex club in New Orleans?" Her eyebrows wag, and her fire-engine-red lips tip into a wicked smile.

She swats the air and chuckles. "Of course, you don't know. You would have told me. There's no way you could have kept it all to yourself."

I'm fucking flabbergasted.

I blink rapidly, too dumbstruck to speak. Sex club?

"It's called Club Sin, and it's just outside town. It's on an old plantation that looks perfectly normal on the outside but is deviant as fuck on the inside. It's gorgeous, elegant, and full of the hottest men I've ever seen. I can't believe I've wasted two years living in New Orleans and never heard about it before," she buzzes gleefully, her eyes wide with wonder.

"Club Sin? Did you go? I can't believe you'd go to a sex club without me," I complain with a pout, ignoring that I wouldn't be any fun at a sex club.

What would I do? Stare? Sip a drink and dance alone at the bar? Those places are fascinating to read about, but I'd be uncomfortable standing in a room waiting for someone to proposition me. I can't have sex with a stranger.

Not yet, anyway.

It's not as if I expect perfection the first time around, but I'd like it to be memorable.

"Why would I go with you? You're a pretty girl, but I don't think of you like that." She sticks out her tongue and smirks. "I went with my neighbor, Jax, the cop. He told me all about it over drinks. After he regaled me with stories he heard, piquing my interest and holding me hostage at the edge of my seat, he had the nerve to say we'd go another time, but I was dying to see it. It's a shame we couldn't go past the lounge. Neither of us were members."

"Jax? The buff guy next door? Did you leave Mack, or are you cheating on him?" I place my elbows on the table and lean closer, hungry to hear more. She's right. This is an excellent cup of tea.

She waves her hand and dismisses my concerns with a shrug. "We had a huge fight, and I finally worked up the nerve to dump him. God knows he's had it coming for months. That dumbass begged me to give him another chance, and when I declined, he threatened to slash my tires. Jax saw the whole thing and came to the rescue. Can you believe Mack? That jerk!"

My jaw drops. I'm stunned Elsa managed to shake that loser off. "Slash your tires? Holy crap, things got rough. I hope he didn't lay his hands on you. My father taught me Systema, and I'm not afraid to use it."

Elsa steals a piece of my cookie and pops it into her mouth, spilling crumbs on her chin as she speaks, "Your dad taught you what?"

"It's Russian martial arts. My father is paranoid and wanted me to be prepared in case bad shit goes down." I end the discussion with a long sip, my eyes shifting side to side as I instantly regret bringing up my father. I don't talk about my family because I don't want to answer any follow-up questions.

The less Elsa knows about Boris Volkov, the better. Lately, I've had a peculiar feeling I'm being watched, and I'd hate to drag her into my messy world. I turn my head and peek behind me, suddenly feeling eyes on me. There's no one there, but the sinking feeling in the pit of my stomach doesn't go away. Perhaps I'm willing my fears to life.

"Why don't you talk about your family? Your dad can't be so bad if he taught you to protect yourself," she says, thumbing through her wallet as her eyes dart back and forth from her purse to me.

"I'm angry with him. It's no big deal, and I'd rather not talk about it." I lean into the table, peering into her giant purse as she ducks her head into the leather bag. "What are you looking for? You've got your entire arm in that purse, like you're Mary Poppins getting ready to pull out a lamp."

I'm too distracted to be curious but eager to change the subject.

"Aha! I found it! Look at this!" She pulls out a shiny black card embossed with gold letters. "Jax and I applied for membership, and they expedited our application. I think it's because he's helped them out of a sticky jam and kept it out of the papers. Places like that thrive on discretion."

"What's that?" Amid her long-winded brag, she's failed to tell me what so great about that card. Or maybe she did. I swear, I've hardly heard a word she's said.

"You're looking at an official member of Club Sin. Jax and I are returning tonight and booking one of the rooms upstairs. That's where all the action takes place," she sings excitedly. "I want you to come with us. As a member, I can bring a guest, and I think it would do you good to get off the computer and live a little. Besides, this is excellent research to improve your content."

She makes a valid point, but I can't envision myself strutting my stuff at a sex club. That isn't a judgment thing. I sell sex, or at least the illusion of it. But flirting online is different than face-to-face. Pinky belongs on the internet, detached from reality, with enough distance to embolden her kittenish way.

No one wants to meet Genevieve.

I swipe the card out of her hand and examine it closely. "Club Sin? What would I do at a place like this? While you're playing with Jax doing God knows what upstairs, I'll wind up alone at the bar wishing I was home making money." I roll my eyes and slide her card across the table, pretending I'm not bummed I can't tag along.

I'm not going to lie. The thought of walking into a sex club titillates me to no end. But I don't want to go alone. It's a shame I've got no one to play with.

Besides, the only men I'm interested in meeting are currently walking the streets of New York, hot as fuck and searching endlessly for a willing partner who isn't shy about taking three dicks at once. As tempting as that might sound, they're there, and I'm here. I'm a virgin who isn't sure she can handle one man, let alone three.

That's way too much pressure for my first time. I need guidance, experience, and a few tricks to slip into my back pocket and pull out when someone loses interest in my tired game. I can't jump into the seedy world of polyamory without experiencing solo dick first.

After that, maybe I'll find I'll be ready for two. Then perhaps, three.

Why am I even thinking about this? I'm living in a fantasy world.

"So, are you going?" Elsa beckons the closest server by shaking her hand, scribbling into the air to tell him we need the check.

I blow the bangs out of my face and huff, too tired to argue and too horny to walk away from an opportunity to get laid. "Let's go shopping. I need a new dress."

Chapter Twelve

Andrei

I'm a stalker.

Believe me, there's no better description of what I do. It's my job to creep in the dark, break into homes, plant listening devices, and lurk in the shadows to watch someone in their most vulnerable state. I won't make excuses or offer insincere apologies for my psychopathic behavior.

It's what I do and who I am.

My business is surveillance, and if I'm being perfectly frank, I enjoy it. Watching people who don't know they're being followed thrills me. It gets me so fucking hard to know I'm in control. I feel invigorated every time I see someone look over their shoulder, tension coursing through their bodies and eyes wide with fear as they sense my presence idling nearby like a predator on the prowl.

I'm good at what I do and take pride in my work. Over the years, anti-spyware and bug detectors have made my professional life difficult, but I've never failed. I've never blown my cover. There is no room for mistakes. I abide by the rules and never compromise my anonymity. Nothing good can come of that. If the person I'm stalking learns who I am, they might connect the dots and figure out who hired me.

These thoughts float through my lust-addled mind while I watch Vivienne Volkov sip coffee with a woman I identified as Elsa Mueller. She's Vivi's only offline friend, and according to my sources, she's a harmless girl who befriended Vivi shortly after she arrived in the city.

Due to my suspicious nature, I performed a background check the moment I learned of her existence, fearing she may be connected to the Grinkov family. Fortunately, her record returned clean, and it was long enough to assume she wasn't operating under an assumed name.

Elsa's a year older than Vivi and moved to New Orleans from California two years ago. I'm glad my girl found a friend so soon after she arrived. Leaving her home and family so suddenly must have been a difficult adjustment. It hurts my heart to think of her alone, fearing she'd be forced to forfeit her future happiness for her family's ambitions.

This morning, I spoke to Boris, hinting that we were closing in on her location but refraining from sharing the entire truth. I'm not ready to tell him everything, and there's no way I'm handing over the information without ensuring he's not planning on betraying her.

He promised those rumors were false, and although I've never known him to be a liar, I can't take a chance with her safety. I'd never forgive myself if I led her into the lion's den, and I'll call on the devil himself before I give her up to someone like Alexei Grinkov.

I won't give her up to anyone.

She's too precious. *Too mine.*

I watch her from across the street, wearing a Tulane University cap pulled tightly over my head and dark glasses that shield a third of my face. The cool morning air allows me to hide my physique behind an oversized jacket while I pretend to be engrossed in a book I purchased on the way here. While I sit outside, drinking, eyes glued to the coffee house across the street, my imagination works overtime. Loneliness can do that to a person.

A server ambles through a side door into the patio area, holding a tray with a single cappuccino. "Can I get you anything else?" He tips his head and places the cup on the wrought iron table in front of me.

A man drinking coffee looks far less conspicuous than a lonely loser sitting in the cold, keeping one eye focused on the girl across the street. I'm already on edge from watching her lush little body walking the streets of New Orleans, unable to hold her close or touch the object of my obsession. I don't need any more caffeine.

As the server walks away, I adjust the volume on my earbuds and continue listening to Vivi and Elsa's conversation. This is a blatant invasion of her privacy and has nothing to do with my assignment. Boris wanted me to find his daughter, not spy on her. He certainly didn't ask me to jack off to the sound of her voice reading erotica. I'm a despicable man. But I'll make sure not to charge him for those hours.

It wasn't an easy task bugging her purse. I lucked out when she stopped in front of a flower shop to admire the pink and purple peonies on display. Vivi brought the bouquet to her face, inhaling the sweet scent before her face grew pensive and sad. I wonder what memories they conjure.

Does she miss her life? Does she miss home?

She's young and undoubtedly feels lost in an unfamiliar place that wants to swallow her whole. It can't be easy being a Volkov. She grew up with one of the most brutal men I've ever met, hovering over her shoulder, watching every move she made. He probably didn't mean any harm. And he certainly didn't mean to traumatize her to the point she no longer trusted him. Boris can be difficult when it comes to considering someone else's opinion. Vivienne was vulnerable, and his protective nature made him want to guard her like the crown jewels.

As much as it pisses me off that he drove her to flee, I can't say I would have been any different. That alone makes me take pause. She doesn't need another overbearing man in her life, and I don't know if I have the patience or strength to loosen the reins.

Vivienne tests my control. As much as it goes against my nature, I don't want to watch her from a distance. I want to barge into her world, gift her with every peony in New Orleans, then declare my love and intentions.

She'd think I was a lunatic, and she'd be right.

I feel insane. It's a familiar emotion I've felt in the past, often when I betrayed my moral compass and killed someone with questionable guilt. Men who pleaded for their lives and promised to do better.

That was a different kind of crazy. It took me to a dark place and changed the shape of my heart for the worse. I didn't think I was capable of falling in love. I didn't think I'd ever deserve it.

Vivienne altered that perception.

My madness for Vivi doesn't frighten me. Considering who her father is, it should. But it doesn't. It suits me perfectly.

Across the street, Vivi and Elsa's conversation grows quiet. I know my earbuds haven't malfunctioned because I hear the irritatingly annoying sound of metal clanking on ceramic. Someone is frantically stirring their coffee. I strain my eyes, struggling to get a clearer picture through the glass, and spot Vivi lost in thought, staring into space.

I'd love to know what or who she's thinking about.

Elsa waves her hand across Vivi's face and shouts, demanding her attention. Her high-pitched cry makes me shudder, and I remove a bud, rubbing my ear to soothe the pain. When I put it back in, I'm flooded with squeals and laughter concerning a particular policeman.

My mind spins with worst-case scenarios as I listen with intent, trying hard to focus on which voice is speaking and who exactly is banging their neighbor. I choke on my coffee, coughing as I muffle my ears with my hands, hoping to drown out the noise from passing tourists.

I breathe a sigh of relief when I hear Elsa's distinctive voice detail her latest adventure to Club Sin, a sex club on the outskirts of town. The name instantly catches my attention, and I whip my phone from my pocket, scrolling furiously through my favorite search engine to verify the location. The logo takes me by surprise. It must be connected to the club in New York. My brothers and I are members but haven't visited since early last year.

Vivi has no business going to a sex club. From this distance, I can't make out her expression, but by the sound of her voice, I can tell she's intrigued. And why wouldn't she be? It's a fucking sex club. It would take a prude or someone on life support not to be curious about what happens inside.

That's precisely the reason I applied for membership in the first place. Curiosity. Fascination with kinks. Exploring my strange proclivities and wondering how many others shared my desires.

It was eye-opening and fun. But it didn't last. As much

as I love a good time and testing my boundaries, boredom came faster than I anticipated.

To truly experience pleasure, you need trust, and trust takes time. I soon learned I didn't want to spend unlimited time with a woman I didn't love. It wasn't long before Vadim and Viktor came to the same conclusion.

We want more than a playmate. We need a lover.

As I listen to Elsa invite Vivi to Club Sin, persuading her to throw caution to the wind and join her this evening, I update my membership and message my brothers.

I think it's time to introduce ourselves.

Chapter Thirteen

Vadim

I stare, fixated, my eyes growing wide as I take in the sight of Vivienne Volkov in the flesh. I didn't believe she'd surpass the image that appeared on my computer screen two nights in a row, but that version doesn't compare to the real thing. She's stunning. There aren't enough words in the English language to describe her beauty.

I've never wanted anyone more, yet there is only a slim chance she'll want anything to do with us. What are the odds her feelings were sincere? The girl has three million subscribers and devoted fans who worship her. We shared a few hours, and she played her part to a tee. Of course, I was swept off my feet. She's good at what she does, which means making every man feel like a king.

That's what she did to me. Meeting her has been the best wake-up call. I know what I want out of life. If we can't win her heart, if she only wants one of us, I know we'll keep trying. Feelings this big won't be contained. Whether this happens now, next year, or five years down the road, I know this is meant to be.

Andrei and I follow Vivi and her friend, watching their movements from the back of the streetcar, standing on opposite corners to avoid drawing any attention to ourselves. Viktor wanted nothing to do with this. He's checked out, preferring to stay at the Four Seasons binge-watching a show he's already seen a thousand times. He's never had a problem sharing a woman. In fact, he was the one who first initiated a foursome five years ago. We've always been attracted to the same women, and in the past, our selfish needs overrode our fraternal loyalty.

We quickly realized some patterns would never be broken. Sharing makes things easier. It keeps us sane and makes us better partners. But Viktor believes Vivi changes everything. We've had relationships, but none of us can honestly attest we've ever been in love.

"Where is she headed? We're almost at the end of the line." Andrei takes a seat near where I'm standing, facing forward while he asks.

"There's a mall a few blocks from Bienville Station. I have a hunch she'll hop off there. You said she wanted to buy a new dress, and there's a place near there with upscale shopping," I explain.

He lifts his wrist to check the time on his watch and then points to the street ahead. "Let's get off at the station and return to the hotel. I don't plan on creeping around while she shops. There are a few things I need to take care of before we meet her at Club Sin. And if things go the way I hope, I'll need some rest."

I drop my gaze and stare at him, bewildered beyond belief. "We can't meet her at Club Sin without talking to her first. I think we need to find a way to let her know that we found her and state our intentions in a way that doesn't make her feel vulnerable or unsafe. If we show up to a sex club unannounced and half-cocked, she'll run for the hills, screaming, fearing for her life.

Andrei shakes his head and looks at me like I've lost my mind. "All members of Club Sin receive thorough background checks. That may be the safest place in New Orleans." He doesn't understand the mind of a woman.

I feel like I've hardly scratched the surface, but I'm trying to put myself in her shoes. Andrei spent too many years as an apex predator and can't put himself in the place of a twenty-two-year-old virgin stepping into a club that caters to sex.

"Head back to the hotel, and I'll find a way to tell her. I've left her a message on the app, but she hasn't answered. I'm hoping she sees it before she heads home. I'd rather not approach her near her house. I don't want her to feel like she's in danger." As the car slows, I step onto the landing and wait for the tram to come to a complete stop. Andrei follows but turns away, keeping the façade that we're not together.

"Fucking Viktor spent forty-five minutes with her last night, listening to her read, asking pointless questions, then cut out early, claiming he had an early meeting. He continues to feign indifference because he's too chicken to admit he's developed feelings for her.

I don't even think he told her he was our brother. If he wants no part of this, I won't spend an ounce of energy persuading him." Andrei hisses, visibly rattled by our brother's lack of cooperation.

He has a habit of needing to control every situation. He can't help himself. He's the oldest son. The responsible one assigned to watch over us by our parents. He took us under his wing when we followed in his footsteps and began working for Boris Volkov. When we wanted out, he took the reins and used the bulk of his savings to fund Balakov Security. We wouldn't be where we are today without his discipline, but he has his faults. He's a fucking dictator.

"I'll see you in a while. Send Vivi a message on the app and let me know if you have any luck," I say as we hop off the streetcar and head toward Canal Street. Fifteen feet in front of us, Vivienne and Elsa giggle as they walk, sharing secrets I can't hear.

Andrei catches me, straining to eavesdrop, and quickly enlightens me. He's still wearing a listening device. "She just asked her friend what constitutes appropriate attire for a sex club and asks if she needs to buy something easy to clean, like rubber."

My eyes narrow with concern, and there's no way to blame my worried expression on the harsh Louisiana sunlight. A storm is brewing overhead, and the sky is turning gray. A sudden thunderclap forces the girls to pick up the pace, and we match their speed until we part ways on Iberville Street.

Andrei waves as he walks away, but his grim expression quickly betrays him. Despite wanting to be the first to meet her, he's aware he must sometimes relinquish control.

A heavy downpour begins seconds after we cross the threshold into an upscale mall on Canal. Unlike my brother, I'm not wearing a hat to hide my face, so I keep my distance, concealing myself behind a heavyset giant hitting the shops with his wife. They tease one another, gossiping about a couple they've invited to dinner who sadly appears to be on the verge of divorce and how much they hope it never happens to them. They're obviously in love, and their easygoing rapport gives me hope for the future.

Would Vivi ever want to marry? And if she does, who would she choose? Would she choose one or all?

I shake my head to clear that thought out of my brain and return my focus to Vivienne. This is the first time I've seen her fully dressed, and clothes do not diminish an ounce of her sex appeal. She's lovely. Sensual. And so fucking adorable.

Her tight black leggings accentuate her shapely legs and the sweet swell of her round ass. I follow, mesmerized by the sway of her hips, wishing I could feel them crashing into mine, rocking to the steady beat of my thrusting cock. She stops in front of a mirror, removes a hair tie from her wrist, and pulls her long dark hair into a high ponytail, making her look like a high school cheerleader on the hunt for the perfect prom dress.

My heart flutters. The steel pipe in my jeans feels seconds from bursting through the seams. While she continues to shop, I retrieve my phone from my coat pocket and pull up the Cam Life app.

> VB731: Hey, Beautiful. Can I see you tonight?

I don't expect Vivi to answer. She's too consumed, wandering from store to store, selecting dresses she quickly discards, unsatisfied with each one. An unfamiliar sting of jealousy surprises me when Vivi lifts a black dress and holds it against her body. Why is she interested in dressing up for strange men? Who does she plan to meet there?

I'm not an indiscriminate voyeur. Andrei loves to watch. Viktor would never admit it, but he's a peeping Tom. When we were growing up, he frequently spied on us with our girlfriends. I'm unsure I ever understood this proclivity until Vivi came into our lives.

I love watching Vivienne. She intrigues me. Fascinates me. I'd follow her without hesitation to the ends of the earth, happily enslaved for nothing more than a third of her heart.

I've never desired that from anyone else.

My mind comes down from the clouds, and I watch her carry a stack of dresses to the back of the store and disappear behind a fitting room curtain. For a moment, I consider leaving. Maybe Andrei was right. My enthusiasm is bigger than my brain. Approaching her at the sex club may not be the most brilliant idea. It may not be any worse than this.

My phone suddenly chimes, and I slip it from my pocket, expecting to find a sarcastic message from one of my brothers urging me to return to the hotel.

> PinkysBedroom: Hi, there. Where have you been hiding? Sorry, I just saw your messages now.

My heart swells with excitement.

> VB731: My brother, Viktor, took the last spot.

> PinkysBedroom: I thought he might be your brother. The three of you have similar features and equally dirty minds.

I inwardly cringe and try not to imagine what he said. In typical fashion, he failed to mention that part of their conversation.

> VB731: Are you available tonight?

I return to my original question, wondering if she'll admit where she's going and hoping I have a chance to tell her we'll see her there.

PinkysBedroom: Have you ever heard of a place called Club Sin?

I'm shocked when she mentions it by name and draws attention to a possible location. With only three clubs currently open and having already admitted she's not in New York, she must know she's made it much easier for us to find her. After all, she doesn't know we already have.

VB731: I know it well. I'm a member. Are you?

Of course, I know she's not, but I can't give myself away completely.

PinkysBedroom: No. But I'll be there tonight with friends.

VB731: Are you in Chicago or New Orleans? Or have you been across the bridge in Brooklyn all along?

PinkysBedroom: I'm in New Orleans, and I wish you were here. I have no one to play with tonight.

I freeze as I read and reread her message. I've done terrible things. Immoral. Illegal. Detestable things that surely guarantee me a place in hell. And if I believed in such a place, I might spend my life in repentance. But somehow, the universe has smiled down on my unworthy soul and granted me my heart's fondest desire.

I'm not letting this chance go to waste.

VB731: Your wish is my command. We'll be there at 9. Look for us at the bar.

Chapter Fourteen

Vivi

"Oh, my God," I gasp and place my hand over my chest, my heart racing wildly as we walk through the velvet curtains and step onto the black lacquer floors of Club Sin. It's exactly what I imagined. The room is dark, luxurious, and filled from wall to wall with the most beautiful people I have ever seen congregated in one space.

"What did I tell you?" Elsa hooks her arm into mine and leads me into the lounge, with Jax following close behind. "Isn't it incredible? The exterior is so deceptive. When Jax and I rode up the driveway two days ago, I was certain we'd taken a wrong turn."

She's right. From the outside, Club Sin looks like the Tara Plantation from the movie, Gone with the Wind. The interior doesn't quite match. It's edgy but elegant. A modern incarnation of a nineteenth-century French parlor room, shag carpets, candelabras, and grand chandeliers twinkling high above, bathing the room in a warm, muted light.

With measured breaths and slow steps, I scan the room

for signs of Andrei, Vadim, and Viktor and try like hell not to get my hopes up. I can't believe how reckless I've become. Not only have I blurted out my location, but I've also revealed my plans for the night. How could I be so stupid? How could I be so needy?

I've met hundreds of men over the last few months, and I've had no difficulty sticking to my boundaries. It's more than simply fearing my father's men. It's a matter of safety. I'm a single girl living in a rough town with one friend whose only life skills are spending too much money on clothes and caring for her feet. New Orleans may feel chill and laid back, but it's no safer than New York.

So, why did I pull such an amateur move?

Because they're hot. They're gorgeous and sweet. Or at least they pretend to be. No one is ever what they claim to be on the internet, and if they do show up, I'll most likely be in for a sad disappointment.

Could I really be that shallow and horny? Have twenty-two years of virginity pushed me over the cliff into a sea of insanity where bad decisions look like clever ideas? This is a disaster waiting to happen.

It's not like I've never been propositioned. I attended NYU for four years, surrounded by hot guys who tried to play grab-ass after they wowed me with a mediocre lunch and a few kind words. That was never what I wanted; each one ended before it began. No one tempted me to lose my cool, flash my tits, or, least of all, show them my pussy over the internet.

What on earth made me do that?

It was Andrei. His piercing blue gaze and seductive voice made me abandon all reason. I felt alive, seen, heard, and so goddamn hot I thought I'd catch fire whenever he called me his baby girl. No one had ever brought that side out in me, and I was sure no one ever would. Until I met Vadim the following night and realized I'd fallen hard for two men in two days.

And then there's Viktor. He's more reserved than his brothers. He doesn't wear his heart—or cock—on his sleeve. I could tell by his blown pupils and the number of times he licked his lips that he'd become aroused during our brief discussion. The longer we spoke, the more he let down his guard and made me want to take things to another level. But the more I flirted, the more he began to pull away.

Is it so wrong if that's what they want? Who are we hurting?

I can't believe I'm considering sleeping with three men. Who does that? Me. Vivienne, aka Genevieve, aka Pinky, is the kind of girl who would sleep with three men. And what better place to do it than a private club dedicated to sex?

By the time we reach the center of the room, I've convinced myself they're standing me up. Vadim said he'd be by the bar, but there is more than one, and it's so dark it's nearly impossible to make out people's faces. Too many men are gliding through tight spaces, weaving between couples, dressed to the nine in couture suits, carrying drinks, and searching for potential partners.

I may be out of my league. There's no way to be the center of attention in a room full of beautiful women. Even if they're here, how will they ever find me?

Elsa takes my hand and leads me toward a less crowded lounge where people seem more interested in talking and drinking than making out. There is a definite air of sensuality and the potential for hooking up, but it's far less intimidating. For a moment, I breathe a sigh of relief and try to calm the terror feeding my anxiety. I'm supposed to be having fun.

Tonight was always supposed to be about research and relaxation. Maybe there's a way to use this club to further my business, setting up meet-and-greets with loyal clients who can pass the club's extensive background check.

"This area is for mingling and hooking up." Elsa points to the plush velvet sofas and high-top tables, each crowded with members flirting, drinking, and discreetly exchanging gold keys hanging on number-embossed keychains. "Only members can book rooms, and unless you're a special case, it's first come, first serve. Jax booked a room for us. We've been experimenting with his handcuffs, and I told him I wanted to try a little bondage," she whispers, peeking over her shoulder to ensure Jax can't hear what she's saying. "He looks serious and sedate, but I swear that man is wild."

I peer past her and take a good look at her man. She's right. Although he appears grumpy, he's been nothing but sweet in the little time I've spent with him. In a room full of beautiful women, he only has eyes for Elsa.

I'm happy for her. She deserves a man who adores her.

I smile to myself and think of what I might do or say if I spot the brothers here. What if they're unhappy with the way I look? Do I present better on camera?

Panic and insecurity strike my heart. My mind spins with memories of awkward teen years, braces, and the unruly eyebrows I tragically inherited from my father. I wrap my arms around my chest, rubbing my biceps as a chill runs up my spine. I suddenly feel eyes on me, and I'm unsure I'm ready. As if the angels heard my silent plea, a passing woman stops inches away to compliment my dress.

"Damn, girl. That dress is on fire. Is that Gucci?" she asks with a drunken smile.

"Yes, it is. You're so kind," I beam, staring down at one of the most expensive dresses I've ever purchased. It's not entirely me, but the vision I have in my head, the elegant, sexy woman I'd like to become. It's called a bandage dress, and it fits like a glove. The tight black fabric holds in and defines my shape. The plunging V-neck with its delicate strappy detail showcases my breasts, held in place by double-sided tape. Elsa gave me that suggestion when I stressed about not wearing a bra. It's fun and feminine with sheer lace at the neck and sleeves and a ruffled hem that gives it a flirty touch.

Despite my father's wealth, I wasn't raised to be extravagant. The sticker price will haunt me for days to come, but it's not every day a girl loses her V-card.

Holy shit, is that what I'm doing? To three men? That's much too excessive. One man will do.

The others can watch. They said they like to watch.

"What would you like to drink? The poor servers are so busy. Jax is headed to the bar to grab me a wine. He wants to know what you'd like before he heads there." Elsa squeezes my hand and gestures to a table to her right, to the handsome men dressed in expensive suits and sipping fluorescent green drinks standing huddled together at a high-top table.

I'm focused on the luxury bar, each swivel chair occupied by men I can't make out, that I don't look hard enough to make out their faces and concentrate on their drinks. I tilt my head and squint, unsure why she's singling them out. But I take a guess. "I think that's absinthe, Elsa. It's too strong for my first night at a sex club, and I'm not crazy about the taste of licorice. Just ask Jax to get me a margarita. I'll Venmo him before we leave."

She narrows her gaze and leans closer, staring at me like I've lost my marbles. "You took so long to decide, I told Jax to bring us wine. Do you suffer from night blindness, ma'am? I wasn't pointing at drinks. I know it's dark in here, but there's enough light to see the three slabs of man meat by the bar. They haven't stopped staring at you since we walked in." She huffs, then discreetly shifts her gaze right, urging me to take a closer look.

Three? I scream the word in my mind. Is this a joke? Did they really come?

"For a few seconds, I thought one of them might be looking at me, but when I stood to kiss Jax on the cheek, their eyes remained fixed on you," she murmurs while adjusting my strap, trying hard to look unassuming. It isn't working. Her slow, calculated movements bring a smile to their faces, and my mortification forces me to look closer.

"I know them," I whisper, unsure if I'm imagining the sight before me.

Oh my God, they're beautiful. Are they really here for me?

"You know them? How? When did you meet three hot guys? And why have you kept them all to yourself?" Elsa slaps my arms, then drops the volume of her voice when she spots Jax returning with our wine.

"It doesn't matter. I think I need to go." I swipe the wine from Jax and empty the contents in a messy gulp that makes me dribble droplets down my chin. I wipe away the evidence and jump to my feet, too panicked to explain my sudden need to move somewhere else, away from their prying eyes, until I figure out what to say, do, and if I really intend to have sex with three strange men.

I teased them relentlessly. Will I be expected to put out?

Why am I acting like that isn't exactly what I want?

"Where are you going?" Jax voices his concern,

searching our surroundings for signs that someone has done something to upset me.

I shake my head, avoiding his questions and urging him to concentrate on Elsa.

"You two should check out your room. Elsa told me it was expensive, and I'm sure you're dying to see what it looks like inside." I dash into a passing crowd headed toward the ladies' room and come close to making a clean getaway. Unfortunately, Elsa isn't letting me off the hook so quickly. She wants answers I'm not ready to provide.

Do they really think I was serious about taking on all three?

I've never even had one man; I don't think I'm ready for three!

"Vivi! You look like you've seen a ghost. You're not going home, are you?" Elsa wrangles me out from the crowd and closes the distance between us, wrapping her arms around me to calm me down.

"No, she's not. She's with me." Andrei appears through a sea of expensive suits and obnoxious baubles like a demon appearing through the fog. He's devastatingly handsome, but that isn't the first thing that catches my attention. His wicked smile turns my legs to jelly. His smoldering gray-blue eyes light my core on fire.

"With you?" Elsa looks justifiably concerned and puzzled.

I nod and place my hand in his, like that was the plan all along. As if I didn't just try to run away and hide in the bathroom until they grew tired of waiting and left.

"Yes. I'm sorry. I should have told you sooner. I'm with them," I whisper, my previously unsteady voice becoming more confident by the second.

"Them?"

Chapter Fifteen

Andrei

V adim was right. I'm happy he told her what to
expect. I'm thrilled she told him where to find
her. Surprising her would have been creepy and
awkward. Three-to-one is bound to be intimidating, and I
want her to feel at ease in our presence.

Lust makes you do crazy things, and my unchecked
enthusiasm could have been catastrophic.

"That is one hell of a dress," I rasp, my eyes locked on
hers as I struggle to regain my composure. She stole my
breath the second I watched her walk through the curtains,
and I haven't found it yet.

"Thank you. Vadim inspired me to go all out. But I
don't think I believed you'd make it here on time. How on
earth did you pull it off?" Vivienne whispers, and her eyes
fall to the floor. Perhaps the intensity of three men staring
with blatant desire is too much for her to handle.

"We have our own jet, and our weekend was free,"
Viktor interjects, his stone-cold veneer slowly slipping
while simultaneously suggesting we didn't go out of our
way. *We were simply in the neighborhood.*

"Your own jet? That must be convenient." Her soft expression betrays nothing. Private jets won't impress a woman like Vivienne Volkov. Her recent excursion to New Orleans may have been the only time she's ever flown commercial.

"We were eager to see you, little one." Vadim can't take his eyes off her. His gaze travels up and down, devouring every inch without being discreet.

She offers a slight smile, her cheeks heating under his lusty gaze, before turning to me.

"Are you happy to see us, or terrified we're here?" My arm slips around her waist as I watch her face for signs that I might be crossing the line.

She smiles and closes the distance between us, nuzzling gently against my chest as if trying to keep her balance.

"Would you like something to drink, or have you had enough?" I ask, though she only just arrived. I know she's not drunk. But I check in, nonetheless.

"I only just started. My friend bought me a glass of cabernet." Vivi looks to Vadim and eyes the glass of absinthe in his grip. "Is that as strong as I think?"

He nods and hands it to her. "Take a sip and see if you like it. It isn't for everyone." She clasps the stem and brings the glass to her lips, taking a slow slip while we watch. Absinthe isn't a run-of-the-mill drink, and we typically wouldn't indulge in something potent, but we're in New Orleans, and the mood felt right.

Vivi's smile widens as she hands the drink back to Vadim. "That tasted better than I imagined."

Viktor's tense expression fades, and he answers her question before she can ask. "I'll grab you one." He darts toward the bar, disappearing into an unruly line of men ordering drinks. I don't know why he's making it so hard on himself. The stranger he behaves, the more I'm convinced he's fighting emotions he doesn't want to feel.

"Are you really from New York?" she asks, still sipping Vadim's drink, her long dark lashes fluttering against her cheeks. I can't believe she's standing in front of us, in the flesh, and ten times lovelier than any other woman I've ever met.

"We are, and so are you, baby girl. I can hear a little bit of Brooklyn in your voice," I tease, still wondering how we'll confess that we used to work for her father and were technically hired to find her. A gentleman would tell her the truth before seducing her, but I can't take that chance.

"I like when you call me that." She's so much shorter than me. She needs to tilt her head to stare into my face. Her gorgeous eyes, bright and as blue as the sky after rain, fucking slay me.

I want to kiss her, hold her close, then carry her to the second floor to relieve her of that blasted virginity.

She has no use for it anymore. If all goes right, it will be gone before sunrise.

Viktor returns with her drink, and as he places it in her hand, they exchange a look I don't recognize. He told me they spoke once but didn't share what they discussed. I despise it when he acts so secretive. He didn't have to come if he didn't want to be here.

"Take it slow. It's as strong as it tastes," he warns her, then practically nudges Vadim away to slide beside her.

She curls into his embrace, and her face tucks neatly into his neck. Viktor wraps his arms around her and whispers in her ear. I can't hear what he says. It's so loud in here I'm not sure she can either. I assume she listened to every word when she nods and weaves her fingers into his hand, clutching tightly, as if they've done this before.

I'm stunned. Vadim looks furious. We don't get jealous over women, not of each other, but there's just something about Vivi that makes us fucking crazy.

I don't know what Viktor's doing or what shenanigans he's got up his sleeve, but I don't like it. Apparently, neither does Vadim. Visibly shaken that Viktor is hogging her all to himself, he wedges his body between them and nudges her back to our side of the table. "Tell me what Vivi is short for? Vivian? Where did you get Pinky from?" We know the answer, but it's best to hear it from her. If this goes where I want it to go, we should know each other's names, birth-dates, addresses, hopes, and dreams. I won't let this start and end here.

"I'm Genevieve. Genevieve Pinkerton." She moves her head from side to side, uncomfortable with her lie and perhaps wishing she could share her truth. Her lips tremble, and I catch her whisper something to herself before repeating it loud enough for us to hear. "But I prefer Vivi."

"You don't look like a Genevieve." Viktor makes a bold attempt to pull the truth, then retreats. "You're definitely more of a Vivi."

I'm shocked by his tact, but I understand his motivation. I have no intention of calling her Genevieve when I'll soon have to revert to Vivienne. We can't keep this charade going for long. Boris expects word from us soon.

Vivi nods cheerfully and leans her back against my chest. I place my hands on her hips and press my stiff cock into the small of her back. A tiny whimper falls from her lips as she peers over her shoulder to face me.

"Daddy..." she purrs the word I've longed to hear.

"I've got a room reserved on the second floor. We can use it. Or we can stay here. The choice is yours, baby girl." My voice cracks with muted excitement. I don't want to tell her how badly I want to take her upstairs. Although my cock is doing an excellent job of revealing my desperation.

Her eyes widen as she wiggles her round ass into my crotch, salaciously rubbing my cock with her cheeks. "Daddy," she breathes. "Are you really going to share me with your brothers?"

I snake my arm around her waist and whisper into her ear. "Is that what you want, baby girl?"

Vivi chews her lip and nods once. "Do you think I'm ready?"

"Daddy will make you ready."

Chapter Sixteen

Vivi

We take the elevator to the second floor and amble through a red hallway, each side lined with black doors numbered one through ten. People pass us in the hall, coming and going. Some look satisfied. Others look eager. No one seems unhappy to be here.

Not even me.

Andrei holds my hand and hands Vadim his key. The Balakov brothers, formally introduced on our way here, give each other a knowing glance like someone has something to say and no one wants to speak up.

"Is something wrong?" I ask, nervous but excited to be alone with them.

Viktor shakes his head and answers, "You can say no, little girl. We want to be here, but Andrei told us this is your first time. Three men is a lot to ask of you. And we want to make sure you don't have any doubts."

"The room is paid for, isn't it?" I don't know why I ask that question. I don't feel obligated to enter. This is precisely where I want to be, and these are the men I want to be with.

Vadim groans, "Screw the money, sweetheart. We don't need to go inside. If you want to join us for dinner, we'll happily take you. There's no rush."

My cheeks heat with embarrassment. "Do you think I'm being too easy? Am I giving in too soon? I want to be here, but if you're unsure, we can go somewhere else." We're moving at lightning speed, but it doesn't feel wrong.

"This is where we want to be. It's not about the place. We want to be here with you." Andrei eases my concerns and urges his brother to finish what he started.

Vadim opens the door to room number nine, and Viktor ushers me inside. Andrei follows closely, examining every nook and cranny of the room, checking behind curtains and closets beneath the enormous king-sized bed, and studying each lamp carefully on a hunt for cameras and bugs. They run a security company in Manhattan, and having suspicious minds is par for the course.

I stride forward, pretending to be fascinated with the décor while struggling to control my breathing. My heart races in double time. My legs shake so hard I fear losing my balance and tripping over my feet.

I run my fingers over the soft velvet coverlet covering the bed and remark on the room's elegance. "Everything looks beautiful. I've never seen a lovelier bedroom."

The room grows quiet. Viktor folds his long legs and falls into an oversized chair directly before the bed. Vadim takes the one beside him. For a few awkward moments, no one speaks. Six eyes focus on me, almost willing me to continue. I don't. I'm not sure what to say in a situation like this.

It's my first foursome. My first time. I'm not sure how things are supposed to begin.

"The room is expensive. The only beautiful thing in this room is you." Andrei's deep gravelly voice makes me weak. "Come here, baby girl. Let Daddy make you feel good." Our eyes meet, and he spreads his arms, welcoming me to his embrace. He's fucking stunning. A gorgeous hunk of man with gray-blue eyes that peer into my soul. I can hardly hold back my excitement, but a few things must be said and understood.

I step forward, then stop, unable to move any closer until they comprehend what this means. I need to lay down my rules. We have no hope of moving forward after today. They don't know my father. I know he loves me, but when he sets his mind on something, very little can change his mind. I don't know why he chose Alexei, but that's not my choice, and no matter what I feel now, I won't surrender my future and allow my secret life to be uncovered.

If I want to maintain a life of anonymity, I can't tie myself to men who live in the same city as the man hunting me down.

"Tonight is just tonight, okay? This can't go any further." My voice shakes, but that doesn't remove the conviction of my words.

No one answers, and the only sound I can hear is the erratic beat of my heart echoing in my ears. Is this a deal-breaker?

I hardly have time to think the words when Andrei storms forward and drags me into his arms. He stares into my face, and his stern expression makes my belly somersault. I don't push away. I make no attempt to struggle or call things off. I fucking want him. Oh my God, I've never wanted anything or anyone more than I want this beautiful man.

"I can't accept your conditions, baby girl. If we start this, I'm not sure I can ever let it end. I won't deny my feelings. And I won't let you run away. If you're hiding, I'll protect you. If you want to create a life with us, we'll build you a fucking palace complete with the three deadliest dragons you've ever met." Andrei wraps his sinewy hand against my throat, then lets it slide to the back. He holds me in place and threads his fingers through my hair, tilting my head back until our lips are aligned.

"What's it going to be, baby girl?" Andrei's warm breath on my lips makes me shiver.

The feel of his cock against my belly sends my pulse into orbit. I try to breathe without tasting the fragrance of his cologne, but his yummy scent wrecks my senses. I'm terrified by his unyielding proposition. I should end this before things become so intense that I run again.

But I can't. It's too late to forget the last five days. And I'm too far gone to leave now.

"I need my daddy." The treacherous words leave me in a rush, like I need to say them before I change my mind. Before I come to my senses.

This is what I want.

Chapter Seventeen

Andrei

It takes almost nothing for me to lose control. I need Vivi. I want her. I need to taste and fuck her. The longer I have her in my arms, the more I long to claim her, body and soul. Unable to control my growing desire, I squeeze our bodies together, pressing her breasts again my chest, grinding my cock against her belly, anything to close the space between us—even if all that remains is air.

"You deserve romance. You should have violins and a lover who takes his time. I don't think I can be gentle. But we won't rest until we lay waste to your virginity and make you come over and over—not stopping until you cry out for mercy." I groan, seal my lips to hers and lift her into my arms.

"Daddy," she moans between kisses, whimpering as she grinds her hot pussy against my crotch. My eyes disappear into my head. She has no idea how much power she has over me. She'll learn soon enough.

"Baby girl, do you remember showing me your pussy?" I whisper as I carry her across the room and onto the bed.

Viktor's eyes narrow. Vadim's lips part. I neglected to tell them about that tiny detail, keeping it to myself until now.

"I do," she cries as I kiss her body. I can't believe she's here, in person, ready to give her daddy what he craves.

"Do you remember when I told you to pretend your fingers were my tongue?" Did I say that? Or just think it? There's no time to second guess myself. While I watch her lying in bed, ready for me, ready for us, I slip my jacket off and toss it to the floor. My cufflinks follow. I'm so nervous that my fingers fumble over my shirt buttons, and I bust through the final two.

"Yes!" she shouts, and the memory comes flooding back.

"You don't have to pretend anymore. Daddy is going to make you come with his mouth. I'm going to fuck you with my tongue until you lose control and come on my face. That's what you want, isn't it? That's what my little girl needs." I shove my hand beneath her dress and pull down a pair of black lace panties, leaving her black stilettos in place.

"Daddy," she breathes, nodding as she spreads her thighs, offering her pussy like a good girl.

I lift her skirt to her waist. I fucking love it when she calls me daddy. She's so much younger than me. I've never been with a woman twenty years my junior, and I never thought I would. If it was anyone else, I'd probably laugh at their idiocy. This feels dirty, depraved, and better than anything I've ever experienced. I'm not ashamed to call her mine. There's nothing I want more than to make her my wife.

"You're my baby girl, aren't you?"

She is. For real. Forever.

Vivi's so delicate. So lovely. She's a flower ready to

bloom, ready to be plucked. I drop my head and skate my fingers along the sensitive skin of her inner thighs. She spreads her legs wider, and I lift them over my shoulders, hungry to taste her pussy.

"I... am...yours, wait, yes!" Her voice falls away and emerges as a guttural moan. I trail my tongue through her wet slit, spreading her lips until I land on the tiny little bud she showed me five nights ago. It's swollen and throbbing, aching for my touch, and I don't make her wait long.

The taste of her sweet pussy blows my mind and taps into a primal need I'm only now discovering. I've pleasured women before. I enjoyed their company and derived satisfaction from knowing I made them feel good. But this is different. Vivi is the treasure I've searched for all my life. The woman I want to please, love, protect, and breed. I want her to be my everything, and I need her to know she'll always be enough for us.

There will never be anyone else.

"Andrei!" she howls as her hips jerk against my face, and I lap harder, devouring her glistening cunt like a man who hasn't feasted in years.

I bury my face between her legs, tonguing her pussy, stroking her clit, suckling that bundle of nerves until she cries out and begs for more.

"I'm so close, Daddy. I'm going to make a mess," she whines, twisting into the sheets as she clutches my hair, pushing me down as she falls into an ocean of bliss.

"Come on Daddy's face, mark my beard with your honey, baby girl. Let everybody know I'm yours."

"Yes, Daddy!" Her head falls back, and her trembling thighs tighten around my face.

I'm not smitten. I'm in love. Desperately, madly in love, I don't know what to do when she finds out the truth.

Behind me, Vadim releases an audible groan and leaves his place at the foot of the bed, crawling onto the mattress to be near our girl. Vivi welcomes him, circling her arms around his neck as his lips crash into hers. While they kiss, I lap up every ounce of her arousal, feeding on her nectar until the scent of her climax obliterates my patience.

Vadim unzips Vivi's dress and pulls it over her head. She isn't wearing a bra, and the sight of her naked breasts makes Viktor crack. He quickly undresses, tossing his jacket, pants, and shirt onto the floor. I don't notice him come closer until his mouth is wrapped tightly around her nipple. Everyone is on her. All of us at once. Vadim and Vik take turns kissing her, kneading her breasts, and driving her into a fit of ecstasy before the last wave of her climax comes crashing down.

This poor girl doesn't know what she's signed up for. She doesn't know what monsters she's created.

I position myself between Vivi's legs and lift one ankle to my shoulder, giving my brothers room to have their way while allowing me full access to her slick pussy. I swipe her clit with my thumb and sink two fingers inside her, priming my path, opening her up for fear I'll hurt her.

I slip inside her, holding my turgid cock at her entrance, waiting for her to look into my eyes before I claim every inch of her tight pussy. "Do you want me, baby girl? Do you want your daddy to take you first?"

Our eyes lock, and she mouths the word yes.

That's all I need.

Chapter Eighteen

Vivi

"I need you to come for me, baby girl. I want you to look into my eyes. I want this pussy to weep on my cock. Milk it dry." Andrei's baritone does funny things to my heart. His words do nasty things to my body. When he talks like this, I can't deny him anything.

I nod, unable to speak but dying to proclaim my undying devotion. I know I said this was a one-time thing, but I had no idea I'd feel this way, that sex could feel this good.

"Use your words, sweetheart." Andrei pets my clit, swirling his fingers across my swollen bud until my eyes hood and my muscles slack, entirely pliable for whatever he wants to do.

"Please..." My mouth is too dry to say more.

He's taking too long and being far too gentle. He looks worried he'll hurt me, but I'm so wet and ready, I can feel my arousal slip down my thighs. He won't encounter any resistance from me.

Hoping to inspire him to let go without openly demanding he fuck me, I wrap my legs around his waist, hitching my calves over his hips and tightening my grip, leaving no doubt about what I need.

Andrei doesn't make me beg. His cock thrusts forward, stretching my vise-like walls with minimal delicacy, bursting through any resistance like a starving man who has just been permitted to eat.

I cry out, my body gripped by pleasure, enslaved by the exquisite way he plays me like a virtuoso.

"Don't stop. Please, don't stop." I struggle to focus on him, but I don't look away, keeping my eyes glued even when I can hardly hold them open.

"Tell me what you need, little girl. Daddy wants to make it better," Andrei growls, his voice low and husky, as he leans forward and seeks the warmth of my embrace. Vadim and Viktor make way, and I extend my arms and wrap them around his neck. I hold him so close I can taste the absinthe on his breath.

He lunges forward and takes my lips, exploring my mouth, deepening our kiss, and feeding our passion. Every kiss fuels my lust and sates the ache in my heart. I don't want to fall in love with three men. Just hearing the words in my mind makes me feel foolish. How can this ever work?

"You're ours, baby. You'll never get away from us."

Without warning, Andrei clasps his hands around my waist and lifts me into a seated position. I look from side to side, unsure of what's happening, until he places me on Viktor's lap. I instinctively fall into his arms, spreading my legs across his thick thighs until I feel his cock slide through my slick folds and nudge my clit.

He's just as big as Andrei.

It must be a family trait.

I hear Andrei's voice behind my ear as he urges me to

let go and do what feels good. "Ride Viktor's dick, Vivi. Do it for your daddy."

I nod and eagerly comply, silencing the voice in my head that reminds me this isn't what good girls do. Desire takes over, and all my fears subside.

"Do you remember what I told you downstairs?" Viktor molds his massive hands against my ass and kneads my flesh as he lifts me off his thighs and places my pussy directly over his stiff cock. I slide down, grimacing with pain as I impale myself on his throbbing erection. It takes a small amount of work and short, concise breaths to work him in, but the growing pleasure blooming inside me makes it worth it.

When he's fully seated inside me, I release a satisfied sigh and nod, remembering his nasty prediction. He promised he'd fuck me second and let Vadim join. We discussed the intricacies last night when things spiraled out of control after a particular filthy reading.

"Is that what you want?" I ask, my eyes cast down as I try to disguise my enthusiastic curiosity to feel two men take me at once.

His hands travel to my waist, and he holds me steady, slamming me down and lifting me up, repeating the motion, bouncing me on his cock with such refined expertise I quickly lose my train of thought and forget my question.

"I want to see you take the three of us at once. This is only the first time, baby girl. You need to know what you're taking on. You should get used to satisfying three cocks at once," he groans, grunting as the friction intensifies with each thrust.

"Now?" A pained whimper escapes my lips, and Viktor slows his pace, believing his passion has exceeded my limitations. It hasn't. His pace suits me. This is the frenzied love-making I craved.

"We have all night. There's nothing to rush," he coos, using one hand to cup my breast and the other to brush the sweaty hair off my face.

"Now," I echo with conviction, hoping he understands that wasn't posed as a question.

There's no hesitation. They were ready for this, ready for me to cave, and prepared to jump on the opportunity. How did they know me so well?

Viktor reclines onto the mattress, clasping my hands to keep me steady, my breasts pressed against his chest, and lifting my ass to give his brother access. Why am I giving in so easily? Why am I angling my behind into position, offering my ass as a tribute to satisfy Vadim's twisted desires?

I lift my gaze and find Andrei standing nearby, no more than a foot away, watching intently, a smile etched on his gorgeous face. My heart flutters, stealing my breath as I prepare for a dual invasion.

What happened to Vivienne Volkov, the girl who was voted most like to succeed at St. Olga's School for Girls?

"Are you sure you can handle us, sweetheart?" Vadim sweeps my

hair off my shoulders, caressing my face as he whispers into my ear.

I nod, whimpering as I feel something slick and cold slide down the crack of my ass. Unprepared and inexperienced, I hold my breath and brace for the pain.

Viktor stills inside me, and his hands travel the length of my back, soothing my nerves as he sighs. "Relax, Vivienne. Close your eyes and let your arms fall beside me."

I listen to his words, repeating them as I feel Vadim's

finger glide into my ass. He starts with one, then adds another, thrusting forward, stretching me open, and tunneling as far as he can go. He's gentle but determined, channeling in and out, letting my whimpering moans lead his pace. Viktor grinds beneath me, pistoning roughly as my lips fall on his in a savage kiss that steals my shuddering breath.

"Tell Vadim you want this," Andrei demands, his voice as stern as his gaze. "Daddy wants to watch."

Viktor unexpectedly pulls out and holds his cock between us, signaling his brother to take his place. Vadim runs his length through my wet slit, dipping in, plunging in and out, with slow, calculated thrusts. Viktor nudges my clit with the head of his cock, and I expect Vadim to pull out before his brother resumes his position. He doesn't.

I'm suddenly aware they're taking me together, side by side in my untrained pussy, whispering soothing words, lulling my panicked mind to accept their dual invasion.

I'm stretched to my limit, filled to the brim with no space untouched. My heart beats in double-time. The breath leaves my lungs. I cry out and grip the sheet beside me while two fat cocks move as one, thrusting side by side, simultaneously grazing a spot that makes me sing.

"Oh, my God!" I wail, spiraling out of control, screaming, clawing, meeting each thrust with the rabid enthusiasm of a porn star.

"You're so fucking tight. But there's something else I want." Vadim runs his tongue across the back of my neck and then grips my nape to keep me in place. Viktor tightens his hold on my hips and jerks me forward, letting me fall into his chiseled pecs. Our sweat-drenched skin feels sticky between us. His pheromones make me weak, perfectly compliant, and willing.

"Relax, sweetheart. This might hurt." Vadim offers a warning that does nothing to stem the tide of my shameless lust. He cups the swells of my ass cheeks, then guides his slick, lube-covered cock into my ass. The searing pain makes my eyes feel as they're flying out of my skull, but I make no attempts to stop him. Inch by inch, I take him into my body until there's nowhere else for him to go

"Fuck, you feel so good." Vadim pumps slowly, his steady thrusts alternating with Viktor's pace. One enters, and the other exits. In and out, in and out, the space between each becomes smaller until they once again move as one. An unbridled pleasure ripples into my core and radiates into my flailing limbs. Their intensity shatters me as one climax overlaps another.

"Daddy!" I focus on Andrei's simmering gaze as his brothers plunge deeper, faster, harder—carrying me away on a storm of lust that shocks me to my core.

"Look at me," Viktor grunts, catching my throat in the palm of his hand as his body tenses and his cock erupts like a hot geyser inside me. I crash with him, my mouth too dry to produce anything but praising whispers as the cresting waves drown me in bliss.

Vadim keeps fucking my ass, thrusting, pumping, his path eased by his brother's seed slipping out from my pussy. He comments on the sight, grunting loudly as he brings me toward him, crushing his lips to mine as he spills hot cum between our thighs.

I'm soaked, marked, covered in the evidence of my descent, and more satisfied than I can ever describe.

"Baby girl, that was fucking incredible." Andrei claps once, and his wicked grin brings a lazy smile to my lips.

I sigh, stunned by my stamina and lost in the naughty afterglow that comes from taking three men together.

Andrei lifts my tired body off his brothers and winds his arms beneath my back and knees. He kisses my forehead and makes his way to my lips, cradling me gently while carrying me to the small shower on the opposite side of the room.

"You were such a good girl," he praises, depositing me on the vanity while he starts the shower. I watch him move, reminiscing on the last hour—three hands, three tongues, and three massive cocks later, I'm happier than I've ever been

Viktor appears at the door, and an incandescent light-bulb bursts in my mind. He moves toward me, his green eyes gleaming with love, but something suddenly feels off. Something he said doesn't make any sense.

I turn from Andrei and hold my hand against Viktor's chest, almost too confused to utter my question. "Why did you call me Vivienne?"

Chapter Nineteen

Vivi

"Stalkers! My father! How could you?" I race across the room with my shoes in my hand and hold the three men I thought I'd fallen for at bay. They lied to me. They tracked me down like a dog, hoping to bring me back to my father.

How could I be so stupid? The writing was on the wall. But I didn't want to assume their Russian background automatically meant they were in league with my father. Brooklyn is full of Russians. Sometimes I can go a whole day without hearing English in Brighton Beach. I know I'm not as dumb as I feel.

"Vivi, please. Hear us out." Andrei takes the lead. "Your father doesn't want you to marry Alexei. He didn't even ask us to take you home. Boris only wanted us to ensure that you were happy and safe. He's worried about you."

My rage intensifies. "How do you know what my father is like? I've known him for twenty-two years and know what he can do. I need to leave. Don't follow me! And don't ever contact me again!" I scream, gather the rest of my clothes, and finish dressing as I head for the door.

"We know your father, Vivienne," Viktor chimes in, still hanging his head for outing their lies. He should feel ashamed. Their trickery is unforgivable. "We used to work for him."

My eyes widen with fear. Only criminals work for my father. "Are you criminals? What did you do for him?" I lift my hand and hold it against my throat, struggling to breathe and too stunned to think clearly.

Vadim hovers close by, trying in vain to soothe my anger but failing horribly. "We killed for your father. You don't know us because he kept that side hidden from you. And we weren't part of the brotherhood. He paid, and we killed. And we left when that life grew too heavy for our souls."

"You left? You left!" I scream, then cover my mouth, fearing someone will knock on the walls and tell us to keep it down. "You're still working with him or for him, whatever you want to call it." I fasten my dress, slip on my heels and turn the knob, swinging it open so hard, it bangs against the wall.

Viktor blocks my retreat, placing himself beneath the threshold to keep me from bolting. He extends his arms, holding his palms out to keep me in place. "I didn't want to get involved with you. I knew this was a mistake."

My jaw drops, and I stumble backward, shocked by his admission. He has nerve confessing something like that when I can still feel his climax sliding down my thighs. "Perfect! Now get out of my way. No doubt my father left New York shortly after you. I may be furious with him, but I don't want him to find me at a sex club."

Viktor remains in place, his soft, remorseful expression spearing my heart at a moment when I need to own my anger. "That's not what I meant, little one. I didn't want to fall in love with you. I fought it every step of the way. We arrived in New Orleans two days ago. I followed you everywhere, watching you, needing you, dying to steal you away so we could keep you to ourselves forever. But that wasn't what was best for you."

"Best for me?" I chew my lip, my voice trembling as I try to offer a sensible reply. "What do you know about what is good for me?"

He steps forward and takes my hand in his. I try to snatch it away, but he's too quick and strong. I don't stand a chance of fighting him off. But he isn't fighting. He's watching me. Waiting for me to let him speak. I should be shocked by their former occupation, but that fact is low on my long list of grievances. I've been around these kinds of men my whole life and know it was what they did, not who they are now.

"You're not meant to be a secret. We won't hide you away. I don't believe your father manipulated us into bringing you home. And if we're wrong, and he did, there's no way in fucking hell we'll let him take you away. We don't think you want to be on the run. You just want to decide your future for yourself. We want to give you that." He threads his fingers with mine and brings my hand to his lips. The soft touch of his breath sends a chill down my spine, and I drop my gaze, holding back tears as I consider his words.

I look to Andrei and Vadim. "What if I want to leave? Will you stay away? Will you tell my father you never found me?" I don't mean it. But I need to know I can decide my future without a man guiding me every step of the way. I've spent too many years trapped in my father's cage. I won't return.

Vadim replies, his features twisted with sadness. "We'll

follow you. We'll wait. You can live your life, but let us protect you from the shadows."

I tilt my head and shift my gaze from Viktor to Andrei to Vadim. My heart aches to believe them, but I know they're lying. They're saying all the right things, wanting me to fall into the trap, hoping I'll eventually forgive them.

"I don't believe you." I sniffle and wipe my tears with my hand.

The room remains silent for a moment, everyone staring straight ahead, contemplating my words and determining their next move. As much as I wanted to get away, my feet stay glued to the floor.

Andrei's husky voice emerges and quickly ends my pathetic standoff. "You shouldn't believe us. We're not letting you go, baby girl. I'm sorry, but we can't. You're stuck with us whether you like it or not." He removes my phone from my purse, hits my father's contact listing and hands it to me. "Now stop being a bad girl and talk to your father. He's worried sick about you."

My rage slowly subsides as I reach the phone and hear my father's voice. "Daddy?"

Andrei's eyes sharpen and his head shakes from side to side. His voice is nothing but a whisper, but I hear it loud and clear. "Not Daddy."

Chapter 20

Epilogue

three weeks later

Vivi

"**W**hat are you telling me, Vivienne? You're deliberately mumbling to keep me from understanding your words." My father grimaces as he takes a sip of coffee, unsatisfied with the quality of the diner's house blend. He's always been a coffee snob.

I clasp my hands and place them on the table, wringing them tightly as I work up the nerve to tell my father I'm marrying Andrei Balakov, his former assassin and the man he sent to hunt me down. He doesn't know I'm aware he hired them, and remains under the delusion I called him of my own accord.

Despite all their hard work and excellent follow-through at Club Sin, the boys declined payment, claiming to have failed in their objective. According to Vadim, it's a low blow invoicing a man after you've railed his daughter six ways to Sunday. I'm inclined to agree.

Three weeks later, and I realized the error of my ways. I should have told my father from the start. At the very least, I should have confessed to meeting them in New Orleans.

I don't know what I was thinking. I can't keep our relationship secret forever. But I do feel the need to roll it out slowly.

"Why are you being so cagey? I don't like you acting frightened around me. You're my little girl. You can tell me anything." My father's pet name sends a shiver down my spine, but I fight the urge to reminisce about Andrei's stern gaze, Vadim's gentle touch, or Viktor's ungodly stamina. It's too soon in this conversation to get derailed by nasty thoughts.

Andrei wanted to do this himself. In fact, he insisted on it. But I couldn't let him. The news won't sound quite as terrible coming from me.

"I have a confession," I mutter, shielding my pink face with my menu. My heart beats a mile a minute, making it difficult to catch my breath long enough to speak. I can't let my fears get the best of me. And I can't expect him to accept it straight away. He's my dad and only a few years older than Andrei. Walking down the aisle with Vadim might have been a better choice. A fifteen-year age difference sounds much more palatable than twenty-one.

It shouldn't have made a difference when I love all three, but Andrei felt like the more sensible choice. He's my daddy.

"Vivi, she's waiting." My real father interrupts my catatonic daze and reminds me the waitress is standing by to take our order.

A nervous cackle bubbles up and explodes past my tight lips. I brush my long locks off my face and slide the menu to the table's edge. "I'll have your grilled cheese sandwich and a bowl of tomato soup. Oh, I'll take a Pepsi with a glass of ice. Please and thank you." I smile wide, my feet tapping furiously against the checkerboard tile while I wait for my father to finish ordering.

My stomach rumbles with nervous energy. Bile climbs into my throat. This isn't the sort of discussion I ever thought I'd have with my dad. I never thought I'd see him again. And truthfully, that saddened me. Since returning to the city, I've neglected to inform my mother of my decision to move home. It's best to remain without contact for now. I refuse to allow her to turn me against my father again.

"Dad, I need to come clean." I start over, buying time before I blow his mind with the truth. He's never going to understand. I just hope he doesn't do anything we'll both regret. I'd hate to cut him off again.

My father's dark eyes gleam, and his mouth curves into a curious smile. "Does this have something to do with Andrei Balakov?"

An audible gasp escapes my lips. "What? What are you talking about? Why would you say that?" Lying has never come easily to me. I'm busted. Plain and simple. But I hate being called out. In another futile attempt to delay what has already been discovered, I attempt to distance myself from the truth.

"Seriously, Vivi? I've known for days, but I wanted to allow you to come to me on your own." He narrows his gaze and waits for me to confess the rest, but I'm too tongue-tied to speak. I don't oblige. "My men saw you and Andrei having dinner at Caravaggio, then walking hand in hand back to his place."

I slump in my chair and hold my hands over my face, hiding my shame in front of the man who gave me life. I'm not even embarrassed about the foursome. I'm humiliated I got caught in a lie. "Sorry, Dad. Andrei wanted to come to you, but I forbade him to take matters into his own hands.

Are you angry? Will you give us your blessing?" I freeze, tilt my head and stare into my father's confused face.

Goddamn, it. I went too far.

"Blessing? For what?" His bewildered expression only makes this more complicated.

I plaster on a fake smile and make way for the waitress. Her sudden appearance buys me a few minutes to get my story straight. He doesn't need to know everything. Only the basics.

"We've got a grilled cheese sandwich and tomato soup for you." The waitress sets my bowl and plate side by side and then turns her attention to my dad. "And I've got a Reuben sandwich with a side of chips for you. Can I get you two anything else?" We shake our heads, and she places a few extra napkins on the table before skittering away. No doubt she sensed the uncomfortable silence between us and wanted to clear the area before things got ugly.

"Blessing, Vivi? You're not seriously considering marrying a man you just met?" He drops the volume of his voice to scold me. I've got it coming.

"We've known each other for a month now, and we're not planning to marry immediately. I just want you to know that's where this is headed. It's serious. I'm in love. Happily, gleefully, madly in love."

He huffs, his fists clenching as he replies, "I like Andrei. Vadim would have been more appropriate for you, considering his age, but Andrei is handsome, and I won't pretend I don't know what you see in him. I wish he had the balls to come to me himself."

"He wanted to, and I said no. I wanted to do this myself." I defend my man from my father's judgment.

This is strange and uncharacteristic. I expected rage, defiance, and threats of death. I never expected resignation.

There's no way I would have imagined him calling Andrei handsome. What the hell is happening? "I love him—" I hold my hand up to stop him from interrupting me before I finish. "I love him, and I understand you're annoyed. He found me, we hooked up, and one thing led to another."

His jaw drops, and his stunned expression makes me believe I went too far. "I don't need to hear details, Vivi. If he's the man you want, then you have my blessing. But understand, if anything goes wrong, he puts you in harm's way, fails to protect you, or breaks your heart, then I will end his life." He's such a bully, but it's the best I can hope for from Boris Volkov.

"If he does break my heart, I sanction his demise," I say flatly. I am, after all, my father's daughter.

"I'm glad we talked about this, sweetheart. I have news of my own, and I need you to be as open-minded as I've been with you," he stammers, his hand shaking as he takes a sip of water. "You may even be happy about it."

My brow creases with suspicion. "That's doubtful. What have you done?" My father is a dangerous man capable of terrible things. I accepted his shortcomings long ago. He was the only stable parent in my life and the only one who truly wanted me around. But that doesn't mean I have to accept everything he does. There are limitations.

"Nothing illegal. I just wanted you to know I'm in love." His gruff, masculine face turns bright red. I've never seen him like this before, and I'm not sure I like it. Love makes you vulnerable, and I don't want him placed in a precarious position protecting some girl.

Plus, I'm not crazy about some tramp stealing my father.

"In love? How long have you known her? Why were you

looking for tail instead of worrying about me?" I slam my palm against the table, then shrink in my seat, fearing I'm making a scene. I don't know what's gotten into me. My mother has never been in the picture, and I'm not accustomed to sharing my father's attention with another woman. Sue me.

His condescending laughter makes me growl.

"Who is she?"

As my curiosity and anger mount, he ducks his head, murmuring something I can't understand, then raising his voice for me to hear a single word. "Sybil."

"Sybil?" I groan, releasing pent-up rage that darkens my reply. "Who is Sybil? In all fairness, you knew Andrei. Who is she? Do you want to marry her?"

He nods, and my heart sinks. I just got him back, and some woman is taking my father away. This is world-class hypocrisy, but I'm too emotional to listen to reason.

"Vasily got himself into a bit of trouble just after you left. He kidnapped a senator's daughter and held her hostage, hoping to make her fall in love with him."

"That is the dumbest thing I have ever—" My father cuts me off.

"I thought so too, but it worked. They're engaged. Her name is Scarlett, and she's Sybil's friend. When Scarlett went missing, Sybil came to me, hoping I'd help find her friend, and before I knew it, I'd fallen head over heels. I've never been happier." He smirks with zero remorse, then takes a bite from his sandwich.

I use my knife to cut a piece of my grilled cheese and then dip it into my soup. While I chew it loudly, I ask, "Is that why you've suddenly become such an understanding father? I expected you to lose your shit over Andrei's age. Is this what happiness did to you?" I'd never begrudge him love and joy. If this chick, Sybil, makes him a better person, I guess I can get behind it.

"Happiness has certainly improved my mood. But Sybil's age doesn't give me a ton of room to judge Andrei," he mutters through bites, then clears his throat with a sip of water. "I understand love is love, no matter how many years you have between you."

His implication sinks in. Confused, I straighten my posture and lean closer to whisper, "What do you mean you have no room to judge? How old is Sybil?"

"She's your age."

I'm dead.

Chapter 21

Epilogue

Two years later

Vivi

Mornings are quiet. Long nights of sex with multiple men are, at best, draining and, at worst, exhausting. And I hate not waking up in my bed. When you live with three men—three husbands who love to take full advantage of marital rights, it's essential to carve out your own place.

I figured that out weeks into our relationship. I couldn't be the only person who didn't have a dedicated bedroom. How would that be fair?

Last night was a particularly busy night. It must have been because I found myself sandwiched between Viktor and Vadim this morning, naked as the day I was born.

They are truly incorrigible.

I slip out of bed, crawling forward to keep from waking them, and reach for my robe. I'm unbelievably sore everywhere that counts and in a few places that don't make sense.

Sore and satisfied. There are worse things to be.

Vadim's snoring startles me, and I drop to the carpet,

fearing they'll wake up and follow me to the shower, always ready for another round.

I'm starving. But sustenance will have to wait until I've taken a few minutes to myself and soaked in a hot bath. I need to clear my mind and give my aching muscles some much-needed relief.

Last night, Andrei brought up the subject of babies. It's not the first time he's mentioned it, and although the others have brought it up on occasion, no one desires fatherhood more than Andrei.

He's forty-five and doesn't want to be too old to enjoy his children.

Don't think I missed his use of that plural word. With three husbands, each should consider themselves lucky. I grant them one each. I'm not a broodmare, but I do want to be a mother.

I tiptoe out of Vadim's bedroom and pad down the hall toward my private suite. Shortly after I returned to New York, I shuttered my platform on Cam Life and took a position at Balakov Security. My husbands may like to watch one another with me, but their tolerance ends there. They didn't appreciate other men watching me, fantasizing about me, and having any kind of peek into my private world.

I didn't fight them on it. Now that I'm back in the city and on good terms with my father, I'm grateful that side of my life never came out. He wouldn't understand. Fathers are like that.

It was Andrei's idea to give me the biggest room in the house, and I'm grateful he did. It's my sanctuary away from the boys, where I can unwind and forget the stress of life. It's like a tiny apartment, a refuge of peace after a long day of catering to three men. Of course, I don't use it half as much as I should.

What can I say? I'm young, uninhibited, and love being loved by three men. I can't imagine living any other way.

I stride into my ensuite bathroom and approach the clawfoot tub, a gift from Viktor after I complained once that my room only had a stand-up shower. It was only an observation. I never expected him to order a bathtub from Turkey. But I'm happy he did. It may be the best gift I've ever received.

"Can I sit with you? On the floor, not in the bath. I know how much you love your alone time." Andrei walks in, dressed in sweatpants and a t-shirt, adorably disheveled. I'm not supposed to play favorites, but if I did, I would probably choose him. I don't know why. Something about him soothes my soul and makes me grateful for everything we've built.

Of course, catch me on a different day, and I'd probably name someone else.

"You can step inside with me. It's big enough for two." I don't need to repeat myself. Andrei always obliges my wishes.

I remove my robe and sink into the hot water. Steam floats around me, and I lean forward, allowing the vapor to cover my face. Between my work and home life, particularly the latter, I never have time to schedule a facial, and I need to take advantage of whatever self-care I can squeeze in.

Andrei steps out of his sweatpants, peels his t-shirt off his chiseled torso, and drops his boxers onto the floor. He lifts his leg over the lip of the bathtub and settles into the other end of the water. He worked late last night and didn't make it home until after Vadim, Viktor, and I had already left for the evening.

"Have you given any thought to what we discussed?"

He waited longer than I expected to introduce his favorite topic—having children.

I nod and grab the soapy loofah floating between us. "Have you thought about how?"

His brows furrow with confusion. "How? I know how to make a baby, Vivi."

I laugh out loud. "I'm aware of your skills, my love. But with three husbands in and out of my bed, I'm not sure I can guarantee which one of you will knock me up."

Andrei's expression grows pensive as he slides toward me and takes the loofah from my hand. He spins me around and proceeds to scrub my back, relaying his plan with tact. "My brothers don't want children. At least, not yet. If you decide to come off the pill, we can take a vacation together, alone, a type of baby-making honeymoon. It should be fun."

I peek over my shoulder and narrow my gaze. "I see you've put some thought into it. Where would we go?"

He stops washing my shoulders long enough to think. "What about Paris?"

I shake my head, unsatisfied with his suggestion. "I can't go to Paris without Vadim. That's our place. That's where we married. It was the first time we were truly alone together. Until Viktor appeared mid-week and crashed the second half of our honeymoon."

His posture sinks. Andrei brings a finger to his lip, his brooding expression signifying he's lost in thought. I lean against his back and relax in his embrace.

"What about New Orleans? We can stay at the Four Seasons. I'll show you my favorite haunts, visit Elsa and Jax then return to Club Sin. For old time's sake we could reserve Room Nine and make some babies. " Although I wasn't originally a fan of his enthusiasm to procreate, the more I fall in love with him, the more I want to build a family.

He'd make a wonderful father.

He's already the perfect daddy.

"Are you giving into my pressure, or have you come around to the idea? I know I'm being a pain in the ass. I know I have issues with control. So don't say yes if you'd like to wait longer. You're my baby girl and will always be enough for me." Andrei dips his head and trails soft kisses along my neck.

Last month I would have jumped at his offer to wait. Not anymore. "I love you. I can't say with any certainty that I'm one hundred percent ready. That level of confidence may never come. But I want to build a family with you, no matter what that looks like. So, yes. This is what I want."

He smiles and winds his arms tightly around my chest. Andrei has never been much for tears, but I swear I hear a sniffle. "You make me happy, Vivi. Happier than I deserve. We're all grateful you came into our lives."

I lift my hand and curl it behind his head, running my fingers through his thick hair, fighting back tears that have a mind of their own. "What am I going to do with you? With all of you?"

"Whatever you want, baby girl. Whatever you want."

If you can preorder Boris and Sybil's story, BIG BAD DADDY, now!

If you can preorder Vasily and Scarlett's story, BIG BAD WOLF, now!

Also by Matilda Martel

DO YOU LOVE STEAMY AGE GAP ROMANCE?

Those are my favorites.

If you like them as much as me,

you might like these titles:

Orphan

My Second Chance

Mile High Senator

Green-Eyed Monster

Takeover

Blindsided

Greed

Get Your Kicks

The Pastor

In Praise of Older Men

My Heart's Desire

Maestro

Gilded Cage

Love Match

Play Right

The Man I Love

Bad Boss

Clever Girl

Chasing Zoe

The Good Girl

My Ward

Do you love Billionaire Romances?

Try these titles:

Takeover

Filthy Rich

Filthy Love

Blindsided

Magic Man

Hostile Takeover

There She Goes

Agreeably Arranged

Bad Boy

Greed

Do you love Friends to Lovers?

Shut Up & Kiss Me

Unsuitable

Lucky Man

Marry Me

Do you love Mafia Romances?

Check out my BROOKLYN BAD BOYS and

CRIMINALLY IN LOVE

Love Interrupted

Love Unleashed

Love Revealed

Vanished in Manhattan

Secret Weapon

BAD BOYS TURNED GOOD?

Check out SCOUNDRELS IN LOVE

Bad Professor

Bad Boss

Bad Boy

PHILLY BOYS FIND LOVE IN LOVE BITES

Love Hate

Love Nest

Love Match

And many more!

Thanks for reading and I hope you come back again!

Stalk the Author

Matilda is a Texas girl in love with a Philly boy who loves to write dirty books about two people who trip into love and fumble their way into a Filthy, Funny, Happily Ever After.

I live in Austin, with my husband, two crazy Chihuahuas and an even crazier cat. And I spend most of my day writing dirty romance books about older men who fall in love with younger women and make fools of themselves trying to win their hearts.

I like my hero to be successful, sweet, suave, sophisticated and kind--- and then I want him to lose all his composure and game when he meets the heroine. I want him to turn into a bumbling idiot when he spots the girl of his dreams and revert to a teenage boy in a man's body trying to win her.

I like my heroines to be witty, intelligent, and unshakeable---who could do just as well without a man—until the hero convinces her otherwise.

I write A LOT OF AGE GAP--because I LOVE AGE GAP ROMANCE. I've got no other excuse for it.

No matter what kind of story it is, my ladies are ADORED, and my endings are always Happily EVER AFTER, not HFN.

To receive a free ebook, join Matilda Martel's newsletter.

Please head to my website to learn what's in the final stages and will be coming out soon!

Made in the USA
Columbia, SC
14 July 2024

38369888R00140